RICHARD HAPPER

365

REASONS

TO BE PROUD TO BE

BRITISH

MAGICAL MOMENTS IN OUR GREAT HISTORY

PORTICO

*To the greatest Brits I know: my son Harry, wife Rachel and father Mark.
And, of course, my mother, Heather. With all my love and eternal thanks, Richard.*

Thank you also to Rory Cook at the Science Museum.

First published in Great Britain in 2011 by
Portico Books
10 Southcombe Street
London
W14 0RA

An imprint of Anova Books Company Ltd

Illustrations by Zoe More O'Ferrall

The moral right of the author has been asserted.

ISBN 978-190755-439-1

A CIP catalogue record for this book is available from the British Library.

10 9 8 7 6 5 4 3 2

Printed and bound in Great Britian by TJ International Ltd., Padstow, Cornwall

This book can be ordered direct from the publisher at www.anovabooks.com

'To disagree with three-fourths of the British public is one of the first requisites of sanity.'

Oscar Wilde

INTRODUCTION

Bold, brave, brilliant and bonkers – the British are all of these things and much, *much* more.

In fact, we're such a diverse bunch of blighters that pinning down what makes us *us* is rather difficult. The English, of course, are internationally renowned for their stiff upper lips; the Scots, however, are known more (much more) for being the 'gallus' type. Many people from Wales and Northern Ireland wouldn't even think of themselves as British at all, considering all the fundamental differences we share – not forgetting, of course, the intense sporting and competitive rivalries between each individual country. So what are we all about? What does it *actually* mean to be British?

I thought that the best (and most fun) way of answering these questions would be to collect and combine a mixed bag of our nation's greatest achievements, historical figures, ingenious inventions, idiotic celebrations, humbling heritage, cultural eccentricities, iconic landmarks, legendary moments and life-changing events and put them in one nifty little book. Then the British – whoever they want to be – could speak proudly for themselves, every day of the year.

When I started researching the entries, I didn't know how the book would turn out – would it be just full of strange and twisted events, peculiar pastimes and kooky, crazy-haired eccentrics? Well, not quite.

As it turned out, us Brits have done jolly well for ourselves, especially considering we are the inhabitants of a constantly rain-whipped, dull-skied, tiny island, floating lonely and unattached off the northwest corner of Europe. Think about it: the British Navy has ruled the world's waves, British sports stars have topped international podiums, British engineers have revolutionised industries and British creative minds have produced and pioneered much of the world's favourite works of art, music, literature *and* technology. Not bad going, at all.

So, without wanting to blow our own trumpet (which is mostly definitely *not* a British thing to do), I present the very best of Britishness here for you to enjoy as well.

So pop the kettle on, tune into the British Broadcasting Corporation on the wireless, settle into your favourite spot on the sofa (or loo, if you're like me) and dip in... I guarantee it'll make you feel proud to be British.

Richard Happer
2nd June 2011

JANUARY

UNION FLAG FIRST WAVED

Is the Union Jack *the* coolest flag in the world? Well, it's certainly one of the most recognisable. An instant design classic that is forever associated with Britain, the Queen and, of course, the swinging Sixties portrayed in every recent Hollywood movie. However, the flag has also become an English stereotype, a symbol that reflects English pride all under one red, white and blue umbrella, or flag, if you want to be specific. Though it is a proud icon of Britain, you'll rarely see any other nation appreciate it quite as much as the English.

And it came fully into existence (as we know it now) on this day in 1801 when the Act of Union merged the Kingdom of Ireland and the Kingdom of Great Britain. The reason the flag looks like it does is because it actually comprises elements of the three individual flags of England, Scotland and Northern Ireland) bundled together. The flag has an even greater history of uniting countries: it has, at one time or another, been proudly flown by 26 other countries, including the United States, and four nations still feature it in the corner of their national flags: Australia, New Zealand, Tuvalu and Fiji.

KIPLING WRITES 'IF'

'If' by Rudyard Kipling is probably the world's most stirring and frequently quoted poem. Its quiet wisdom, a reflection on the beauty of living a virtuous and humble life adorns office walls, is spoken publically at major rallies and is displayed at countless public monuments across the land. It even is framed on the wall of the players' entrance to Centre Court at Wimbledon. It is the quintessential English poem written by a very English poet.

Kipling was inspired to write the inspirational verse after a colonial raid executed by Sir Leander Starr Jameson in the Transvaal province, South Africa which finished on this day in 1896. The raid was a bloody disaster and its failure helped incite the Second Boer War. Still, the poem is jolly nice.

THE IRON LADY'S SOFTER SIDE

When Margaret Thatcher became the longest-serving Prime Minister of the 20th century today in 1988, it defined an era of intense British political history. And, while her politics might have divided the nation (and still do), we can all unite in appreciation of her *other* major contribution to British life: as a young graduate chemist, she helped perfect the soft-style ice cream dispensed on tap in ice-cream vans.

ALL RISE FOR ROSE

Rose Heilbron helped bring Britain into a new age (perhaps long overdue) of sexual equality today in 1972 when she became the first female judge to sit at the Old Bailey. She was a role model for British women in many respects, becoming the first female King's Counsel in England and the first to lead in a murder case.

WILLIAM SMITH'S GEM OF AN IDEA

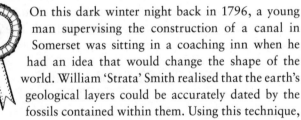

On this dark winter night back in 1796, a young man supervising the construction of a canal in Somerset was sitting in a coaching inn when he had an idea that would change the shape of the world. William 'Strata' Smith realised that the earth's geological layers could be accurately dated by the fossils contained within them. Using this technique, he produced the first geological map of Britain and the concept of mapping strata (a layer of sedimentary rock) has now become indispensable to oil, gold and diamond exploration. Smith is now affectionately referred to as the 'Father of English Geology' – which would then make Mother Nature his wife, surely?

STONES START TO ROLL

Mick, Keith and the rest of the Rolling Stones rolled out of London on their first headline UK tour today in 1964, supported by The Ronettes. This is the tour that broke the band on a national level, following hot on the heels of another successful British beat combo called The Beatles (or something). Originally, the Stones were deemed just another blues cover band, but their inspired early songwriting (their first hit was, in fact, written by Lennon & McCartney) and enthralling live act helped shape the exciting 60s London scene, before becoming the most long-lived and influential British band of all time. And to think, Mick and Keef met, by chance, on a Dartford train in 1961.

THE FIRST FILM STAR

The prodigious American inventor Thomas Edison invented motion picture production, right? Well, many of his most important breakthroughs were actually made by William Dickson, a Scottish inventor who worked for Edison's company. Dickson built an early motion picture camera and initiated 35mm film, which he patented today in 1894, as the industry standard. And it still is.

THE TWO QUEENS

Luxury ocean liners are a proud part of British heritage that has seen a recent resurgence in popularity. When the Cunard RMS *Queen Mary 2* was christened by the Queen at Southampton Docks today in 2004, she was the largest, longest, widest, tallest and most expensive passenger ship ever built. At 151,400 gross tons, 1,132 feet long and with room for 3,056 passengers, she was the largest ocean liner ever built. Though, no doubt, by the time you read this that record would have been smashed again.

LET THERE BE LIGHT

Before this day in 1816, the naked flames of miners' lamps caused many tragic, though somewhat obvious, methane explosions. Then Cornish chemist Humphry Davy introduced his safety lamp, which used a fine metal mesh to diffuse the flame's heat and prevent ignition of mine gases.

Strangely enough, the widespread introduction of the 'Davy Lamp' actually increased accident figures, as mines previously considered too dangerous to work because of potential gas explosions were reopened. Whoops.

WORLD'S FIRST UNDERGROUND

10 Next time you're strap-hanging in 100-degree heat on the Circle Line, don't despair, take pride! You are travelling on a pioneering marvel of transportation – the world's first underground railway line. The Metropolitan Railway opened today in 1863 and originally took delighted passengers only between Paddington and Farringdon. But the Tube (as it later became known) soon expanded across London, while its idea and name spread to other countries. The Tube is still one of the biggest metros in the world with 270 stations, 250 miles of track and more than a billion passenger journeys each year.

YE NATIONAL LOTTERY

11 Our national love for the lottery actually has a long history – the first was chartered by Queen Elizabeth I and drawn today in 1569. This aimed to raise money for the 'reparation of the havens and strength of the Realme, and towardes such other publique good workes'. The government deficit, in other words. The government later went on to sell lottery ticket rights to brokers, who then hired agents and runners to sell them. These brokers eventually became modern-day stockbrokers. So, next time you play the lottery and don't win, blame them.

FOR EVER, FOR EVERYONE

When social reformer Octavia Hill, solicitor Robert Hunter and clergyman Hardwicke Rawnsley got together today in 1894 to form a preservation society, they could hardly have imagined how successful they would ultimately be.

Now their creation, the National Trust, has saved and restored many of Britain's beloved buildings from ruin, or worse, sold to the highest bidder. The Trust now owns 200 historic houses, 630,000 acres of land (nearly 1.5 per cent of the total land mass of England, Wales and Northern Ireland) and has 3.7 million members.

A BREATH OF FRESH AIR

Before Irishman Sir Francis Beaufort devised his Wind Scale today in 1806, one sailor's hearty breeze was another's roaring gale. And hurricanes are bad enough without that sort of confusion.

Beaufort not only standardised storm ratings, he was also a first-class hydrographer who made sea charts so accurate they are still being used 200 years later. He also sent biologist Charles Darwin off on his *Beagle* voyage to the Galapagos Islands, where his wind-force scale was used officially for the first time.

SLIDING INTO HISTORY

14 The British don't have alpine weather, as such, but we did help create many modern winter sports. Well-to-do Victorian gents wintering in St Moritz, Switzerland began bolting delivery boys' sledges together and racing them down the town's ice-packed roads, so creating bobsleighing (or tobogganing, if you prefer). And today in 1885 the famous, or should I say notorious, Cresta Run was opened. The track is 1,212m (3,978 ft) of ice and is one of the few bobsleighing tracks dedicated to skeleton sledging. It is owned and operated by the male-only 'Cresta Club' whose daring members are largely still British gentlemen.

THE NEW MUSEUM

15 The British Museum opened its stately doors for the first time today in 1759. Established by the bequest of collector Sir Hans Sloane, it was the first of a new kind of museum: owned by the nation, free to all, and aiming to collect *everything*. The museum now has more than seven million objects and artefacts, making it one of the most comprehensive records of human culture in the world.

TOP HAT AND TALES

The story goes that, today in 1797, a haberdasher called John Hetherington was arraigned before the Lord Mayor of London on a charge of breach of the peace and inciting a riot. His crime? Venturing out in public wearing the first top hat. Officers stated that 'several women fainted at the unusual sight, while children screamed and dogs yelped'. Believe it or not, but fashion always has been a dangerous business.

HOW'S THAT?

Cricket may have its slow moments (and I'm being kind here), but that just makes it one of the few sports where you can go and queue at the bar for twenty minutes and not really miss much. Now the world's favourite bat-and-ball game (it has a much more international appeal than baseball), its history stretches way back to Tudor England, with the first mention of the sport recorded on this day in 1598, referred to as 'creckett', and in a court case, no less.

GREAT SCOTT

We Brits love the plucky underdog, and no one personifies that more than Devonshire man Robert Falcon Scott. Fiercely determined, brave, headstrong and ultimately eloquent in the face of death, he became a great British hero for his expedition to the South Pole just *one* month after Roald Amundsen. However, Scott discovered his rival's tent at the bottom of the world first and turned for home, dejected, today in 1912. After two more months slogging back across the snow in savage conditions, his team perished within 11 miles of safety.

WATT A CLEVER BOY

Scotsman James Watt (born today in 1736) perfected something that would transform human existence more than any other innovation – the steam engine. The Newcomen engine was already in use, but was very inefficient and only used as a pump. What Watt did was make some brilliant improvements – his engine used 75 per cent less coal than Newcomen's. It could also produce a rotary motion, to drive factory machinery and wheels. Watt's steam engine very quickly began replacing water wheels and horses as Britain's main source of mechanical power and the Industrial Revolution was under way.

I CALL THIS HOUSE TO ORDER

Simon de Montfort was a nobleman who rebelled against Henry III and became, briefly, acting ruler of England. He called on elected representatives from every county in England to meet at Kenilworth, Warwickshire which they did today in 1265. Although it was dissolved within a month, and de Montfort would be killed at the Battle of Evesham later that year, this created the first directly elected parliament in medieval Europe and made de Montfort one of the fathers of modern democracy.

DELOREAN TIME MACHINE

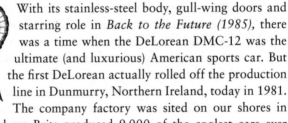

With its stainless-steel body, gull-wing doors and starring role in *Back to the Future (1985)*, there was a time when the DeLorean DMC-12 was the ultimate (and luxurious) American sports car. But the first DeLorean actually rolled off the production line in Dunmurry, Northern Ireland, today in 1981. The company factory was sited on our shores in 1978 and we Brits produced 9,000 of the coolest cars ever designed by man ... before DeLorean went bust in 1982.

AND THE CROWD GOES WILD ...

22 Football fans the world over got a new treat today with the first ever live radio commentary on a match, between Arsenal and Sheffield United at Highbury. The year was 1927. To accompany the broadcast *The Radio Times* published a pictorial grid of the pitch divided into eight squares to help listeners place the ball as the commentary was spoken. One theory states that the origin of phrase 'back to square one' was coined by one of the commentators during this match.

THEY'RE COUNTING YOUR GUNS ...

23 The Battle of Rorke's Drift, 1879 was one of the most heroic episodes in British military history. A group of just 139 soldiers successfully defended their garrison against around 4,000 attacking Zulu warriors. Only 17 men died during the 10-hour onslaught, combining gun battles and hand-to-hand fighting, and 11 Victoria Crosses were awarded in the aftermath. This battle was immortalised in the 1964 film *Zulu*, starring England's Chief Gent-at-large Michael Caine in his first role.

SCOUT AND ABOUT

Lord Robert Baden-Powell was a Boer War hero who was impressed by the ability of young lads to act as scouts and messengers in the war in Africa. He believed their resourcefulness and initiative could be encouraged in civilian life. On his return to England, he put his ideas into practice at a camp in Dorset and today in 1908 published a world-changing book, *Scouting For Boys*. Now more than 28 million people worldwide enjoy scouting, making it one of Britain's most enduring, and famous, exports.

SAY 'CHEESE'

Frenchman Louis Daguerre is often thought of as the father of photography, but Dorset-born William Talbot is actually the daddy. Talbot had been taking photographs for five years when Daguerre exhibited his first pictures in early 1839. Talbot promptly showed his five-year-old shots at the Royal Institution on this day. And, where Daguerre used cumbersome sheets of copper, Talbot used the more flexible negative/positive paper process and required much shorter exposure times. This was Talbot's invention – the Calotype process.

RUGBY KICKS OFF

26 Normally, picking up the football and running with it during a school game would get you a thumping from your team mates, but for English lad William Webb Ellis it earned him the reputation as the inventor of an entirely new sport – rugby. The first league was inaugurated today in 1871, and now millions of egg-chasers worldwide devote themselves to the game, which also influenced the development of American football, Canadian football and Australian rules football.

JETS TAKE OFF

27 Today we celebrate the man who is responsible for more happy holidays happening than anyone else. No, not Walt Disney – the engineering genius Sir Frank Whittle. On 27 January 1936, a company called Power Jets Ltd came into being. This little-known venture aimed to develop and manufacture Sir Frank's world-shrinking invention, the first ever jet engine. He succeeded and it's been 'a small world after all' (to quote Walt Disney) ever since.

ROAD SAFETY GETS INTO GEAR

Petrol-heads won't be feeling very proud today, but the rest of us can be pleased. On this day in 1896, the first speeding conviction was handed out, to Walter Arnold, who was clocked at a giddy 8 mph. The limit was then 4 mph, and Walter was fined one shilling plus costs. He could put his foot down later that year though, when the Locomotives on Highways Act 1896 raised the speed limit to a head-spinning 14 mph.

NO, YOU CAN'T HAVE A BOAT

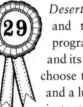

Desert Island Discs is a British cultural institution and the world's longest-running, factual radio programme. It was first broadcast today in 1942 and its simple but intriguing format – famous people choose their eight favourite pieces of music, a book and a luxury item to be cast away with – became an instant listening hit. More than 22,000 discs have been chosen over the last 70 years, the most popular of which is Beethoven's 9th symphony. Though, Mozart is the most requested composer.

LYING IN STATE

30 Today in 1965 may have seen the end of the great man, the noble, wise and beloved Winston Churchill, but it was the beginning of his enduring legend. Britain's charismatic leader not only helped the Allies defeat the Axis powers in World War Two, he was also an eminent soldier, historian, artist and the only British Prime Minister to a) be elected Prime Minister *twice* and b) win the Nobel Prize in literature. As such, he was one of the very few civilians in British history ever to be given a state funeral and is an archetypal British figurehead synonymous with our bulldog spirit and plucky determinism.

CUTTING-EDGE CLINIC

31 Not an overly proud reason to be British, this one, but an interesting one nonetheless in Britain's history of being the global trendsetter...

The world's first hospital for tropical diseases (much, *much* more exciting than it sounds), the London Lock Hospital (in Grosvenor Place), was the world's first specialist venereal disease clinic, and it opened on this day in 1747. It was opened to counter the scourge of syphilis that had become rife on our shores in the sixteenth century – now that adventurers in their fancy ships were sailing all over the world looking for new exotic locations to set up colonies. The hospital's name actually derived from the term 'locks', or rags, that lepers used to wear. Lovely.

FEBRUARY

THE ORIGINAL SURVIVOR

Today in 1709, Scottish sailor Alexander Selkirk saw his first human being in four years and four months. He had been cast away (at his own request – he doubted the seaworthiness of the ship he was sailing on) on the uninhabited island of Juan Fernández off the coast of Chile and had survived alone by eating wild goats and native plants. He returned to Britain and became the inspiration for Defoe's famous *Robinson Crusoe,* the original survival story.

SKY'S THE LIMIT

Despite inventing the television, and the mighty institution that is the BBC, us Brits were slow to realise that there might actually be an audience for such ridiculous televisual treats as extreme wife swapping. So, it wasn't until today in 1989 that the Rupert Murdoch-owned Sky TV launched and we finally had a *much* wider choice of top entertainment.

GOING UNDERGROUND

Early London Tube maps were scaled to show the correct distances between stations. Most of the suburban space was wasted, and the busy central area looked very cramped. Then draftsman Harry Beck realised that travellers only needed to know the order of stations and where to change. He threw spatial correctness out of the window and today in 1931 produced the representational Underground map. London Transport (and the world) got a design classic. Harry got 10 guineas.

BATMAN, BOURNE & BOND

Pinewood (in Buckinghamshire) is one of the world's major movie studios, the birthplace and filming location of hundreds of celluloid classics including *Chitty Chitty Bang Bang*, *Oliver Twist*, *Bugsy Malone*, the *Carry On* series, *Batman*, *Bourne* franchise and most of the 22 James Bond adventures. *London Melody* was the first film made there, and was released today in 1937.

GOLDEN NUGGET

British people have always had a knack for making big discoveries and, today in 1869, two Cornishmen made a whopper. John Deason and Richard Oates were mining near Moliagul in Australia when they dug up the world's largest gold nugget. It measured a mighty two feet wide by one foot broad and weighed 3523.5 troy ounces. The canny Cornwall lads found it just 2 inches below the surface, by a tree root, and dubbed it the 'Welcome Stranger'. It earned them £9,000 – equivalent to £430,000 today, although it would be worth £2 million at today's gold prices.

SINGAPORE SLUNG

6

If you're going to start a colony, it's always a good idea to do it somewhere warm where you can make lots of money by trading and amuse yourself by shooting wildlife. Well, that was Sir Thomas Stamford Raffles' plan anyway, when he founded Singapore today in 1819.

The famous Raffles Hotel named after him is not only where the infamous cocktail Singapore Sling was invented, it was also where the last of the island's wild tigers was shot – in the Long Bar in 1902.

GET IN THE RING

7

What does American John L. Sullivan becoming world heavyweight boxing champion today in 1881 have to do with Britain? Well, this was the first battle for a world belt under the Marquess of Queensberry rules. The new code, which included the use of gloves, the ten-count and three-minute rounds, had actually been written in 1865 by John Graham Chambers and published two years later under the patronage of John Douglas, 9th Marquess of Queensberry. It superseded a more brutal set of rules and gradually became the established conduct for all future fights.

27

CANINE CRIME-FIGHTING

8 This winter's morning dawned bleak and damp on a Scottish moor back in 1816, but it also ushered in a bright-eyed (and cold-nosed) new era of law enforcement. It was up to Revenue Officer Malcolm Gillespie to catch gangs of whisky smugglers as he tramped across the braes of Aberdeenshire. It was hard, dangerous work and he had the brilliant idea of using a dog to help sniff out the contraband. His tactic seemed barking mad but it worked and Gillespie had started a whole new branch of using canines to fight crime.

POP TO THE TOP

9 Will Young or Gareth Gates? If you know what that question means, then you'll probably be interested to hear that the first TV *Pop Idol* was crowned by the British public tonight in 2002. The show went on to dominate Saturday night light entertainment TV all over the world, with countless international spin-offs and franchises, as well as bequeathing its addictive format to global behemoth *The X-Factor* – still one of the most highly watched TV shows in Britain (and the world).

WHAT THE DICKENS?

Charles Dickens is one of the best-selling novelists in British history and the creator of some of the most memorable characters in literary history, including Oliver Twist, Ebenezer Scrooge, David Copperfield, Mr Micawber, Miss Havisham and Uriah Heep. There have been more than 180 film and TV adaptations of his works. It was today in 1836, however, that Dickens' first novel *The Pickwick Papers* was commissioned as a monthly serial. It was an immediate success, bringing the 24-year-old writer instant recognition and inspired him to go on and write a whole catalogue of classic characters that are as part of the British landscape as the white cliffs of Dover.

SCI-FI LANDS ON TV

Way back in 1938 on this day, BBC Television had an eye on the future when they produced the world's first ever science-fiction television programme. This was a 35-minute chunk of the Karel Capek play *R.U.R.*, set in a factory that made artificial people. This play is notable as it coined the term 'robot' – R.U.R. stands for Rossum's Universal Robots.

UNHAND OUR FISH, FROGGIES

12 Britain enjoys a generally good relationship with France (they have such lovely wine, after all), but occasionally they need to be taught a lesson. Take today in 1429, when an English force was quite innocently besieging the town of Orléans. The French then had the audacity to intercept a vital supply convoy of barrels of herring (admittedly, there might have been some crossbows and cannons in there too). This was simply too much. Seriously miffed by this misappropriation of their elevenses, our lads promptly won the resulting 'Battle of The Herrings'.

IN THE PINK

13 The *Financial Times* was first published today in 1888 as a four-page journal aimed at 'The Honest Financier and the Respectable Broker'. A modern cynic might wonder how it ever found a market, but it did, and its distinctive salmon-pink pages are now perused by half a million respectable (and not-so-respectable) moneymen around the world every working day.

YE OLDE VALENTINE

British people are very rarely associated with being romantic but there is evidence to suggest otherwise. Valentine's Day is popular with lovers around the world (and with greetings cards companies) and the first recorded link of St Valentine's Day with romantic love is in Geoffrey Chaucer's *Parlement of Foules*, published in 1382. The practice of sending romantic cards to loved ones on this day became hugely popular in Britain in the late 18th century, and subsequently spread to other affectionate countries.

DECIMAL DAY

We held on as long as we could. The decimalisation of sterling had been proposed as early as 1824, but it wasn't until today in 1971 that Britain did away with the most confusing – yet charming – monetary system the world has ever seen.

There were 240 pence in a pound, 12 pence in a shilling and 20 shillings in a pound. There were also farthings (a quarter of a penny), florins (two shillings) and half-crowns (two shillings and sixpence). Tourists were utterly bamboozled by it all – how fabulous!

THE WINGS OF AN ANGEL

16 Although it met with quite a bit of resistance before it was built, artist Antony Gormley's *Angel of the North* has since become one of Britain's favourite landmarks. Construction of the 66-foot-tall steel sculpture was finished today in 1998. Its famous wings stretch for 177 feet and weigh 50 tonnes each. Locally, the *Angel* is often affectionately referred to as the 'Gateshead Flasher'.

TURNING YOUR CAR INTO CASH

17 Not the most popular British innovation if you simply fancy driving around the capital's sights, but the London Congestion Charge (introduced today in 2003) has been one of the world's most successful such money-rasing ventures. It has also lowered accidents and emissions in the city, and raises around £90 million a year to help fund Mayor Boris Johnson's other mad (but excellent) schemes. Curiously, the US Embassy has refused to ever pay the congestion charge, racking up a total of £3.44 million of unpaid bills to date.

MAKING PROGRESS

The Pilgrim's Progress by Bedfordshire-born John Bunyan is one of the most famous and influential books in world literature and it was first published today in 1678. Its poignant Christian allegory has inspired countless other writers, has been translated into more than 200 languages and has never been out of print. Many of Bunyan's creations, characters, places and phrases have become proverbial, including the 'Slough of Despond', 'Vanity Fair', 'House Beautiful' and 'worldly wise'.

NEW YORK, NEW AMSTERDAM

Today in 1674, England and the Netherlands signed the 'Treaty of Westminster', ending the Third Anglo-Dutch War. It might sound like the end of an unremarkable – OK, boring – trade dispute but, crucially, it ceded the then Dutch colony of New Netherland to England. It's then-capital, New Amsterdam, was promptly renamed New York. Much better. And, of course, many millions of British people have been travelling to New York ever since. Though, these days, it's mainly for the *haute couture*, Broadway and the breathtaking skyline.

PREMIER LEAGUE FORMED

20 The English Premier League is the world's most-watched soccer league and, in turn, the most lucrative. The idea first kicked off today in 1992 when clubs in the Football League First Division broke away from the Football League to take advantage of a juicy television rights deal. Of the 44 clubs who have played in the Premiership, only four have won it: Manchester United, Arsenal, Chelsea and Blackburn Rovers.

BOUDICCA'S BONES

21 Warrior Queen Boudicca was one of the earliest of all British heroes, leading a major uprising against occupying Roman forces in AD 60. And, today in 1988, archaeologists found what they thought could have been her grave – under platform 8 at King's Cross station. Of course, it might just have been a commuter still waiting for the six o'clock to Peterborough, but it's a nice story.

BAA BAA CLONED SHEEP

 You might think that, since sheep are hard enough to tell apart at the best of times, the last thing you want is two that are absolutely genetically identical. But the cloning of Dolly, which was announced today in 1997, was a terrific British scientific achievement and one that delighted the world – Dolly was the world's first cloned mammal.

ONE JOLLY CAREFUL OWNER

 In the days before eBay, people bought stuff they didn't really need (or use again, come to think of it) from classified adverts published in the back pages of newspapers. These first appeared today in Britain in 1886 in the pages of *The Times*. They still exist today but, sadly, not for much longer you would imagine.

THE MCFLYER

Today in 1923, the now-famous Flying Scotsman locomotive first steamed into service. It became world famous for becoming the first steam engine train to top 100 mph, and being able to run non-stop between London and Edinburgh – at 392 miles, the longest express route in the world. It was named after the actual scheduled service linking the two cities, which started in 1862.

THE FIRST OF MANY F-WORDS

Britain currently has more TV chefs than you've had hot dinners, and Gordon Ramsay is undoubtedly their king, showcasing the UK phenomenon that is TV chefs to the world. He first swore his way into the national consciousness today in 1999 when his documentary *Boiling Point* was broadcast. This show followed the foul-mouthed chef during eight of the most intense months of his life as he opened his first restaurant in Chelsea. This would ultimately earn him the highly prestigious (and incredibly rare) three Michelin Stars ... and establish him as the best British bistro bully boy bar none.

FIRST GRAND NATIONAL RUN

Every year, more than 500 million people tune in to watch their sweepstake pick blunder into the first hedge during the Grand National, the world's greatest steeplechase.

The gruelling Aintree race covers 4 miles and 856 yards and throws up 30 fences. It was first run today in 1839 and was won, fittingly enough, by a horse called Lottery.

LOTTERY

BANG BANGS KISSED BYE-BYE

27 The passing of the British ban on handguns today in 1997 was bad news for our Olympic pistol squad (they subsequently had to practise abroad), but pretty good news for those of us who don't want to get shot. It may be one of the world's most restrictive gun laws, but then Britain also has one of the world's lowest rates of gun homicides.

THE SECRET OF LIFE...

28 Today in 1953, two Cambridge scientists wandered into the town's Eagle pub and announced, 'We have found the secret of life.' James Watson and Francis Crick weren't talking about best bitter (though they weren't far off!), they meant they had just decoded the structure of deoxyribonucleic acid (or DNA to you and I). Their discovery that life's hereditary genetic information is structured in a double-helix set the foundations for incredible advances in molecular biology and gave us greater understanding of the human body and how life is able to occur.

MARCH

CELEBRATING ST DAVID

Today is St David's Day, chosen in remembrance of the death of St David, patron saint of Wales, in 589. This makes it a fitting day to celebrate one of the most remarkable places in Britain and the saint's final resting place: St David's or, to give it its official name, 'St David's and the Cathedral Close'. This is the smallest city in Britain, located in Pembrokeshire, and has a population of just 1,797.

MONEY MONEY MONEY

We may have simplified our currency a bit with decimalisation, but our paper money is still wonderfully, eccentrically British. To summarise: Bank of England notes (which first appeared today in 1797 in £1 and £2 denominations) are legal tender in England and Wales; Scottish and Northern Irish notes are not, but may be accepted at the vendor's discretion. In Scotland and Northern Ireland, no banknotes at all, not even ones issued in those countries, are legal tender. They are, of course, accepted, but really only have the same standing as cheques.

TO BE OR NOT TO BE … THE BEST

William Shakespeare is widely regarded as not just the greatest writer in the English language, but also the world's pre-eminent dramatist. He is also the bestselling author of all time, shifting around 4 billion copies of his plays and poetry. The earliest date we have for a production of one of his plays is today in 1592 when *Henry VI Part I* was first performed.

FOR THOSE IN PERIL ON THE SEA

The Royal National Lifeboat Institution (RNLI) was founded on this day in 1824. It was the idea of Sir William Hillary, who believed a national lifeboat service manned by trained crews would be a huge benefit to seafarers and to the country, especially as Britain is an island surrounded by *lots* of water. He was right – the RNLI's crews have saved over 137,000 lives over the years. In 2009, its fleet of 444 boats rescued an average of 22 people a day.

SPRAY TO GO

To some, he's a mindless vandal destroying the beauty of our cities; to others, he's a ground-breaking British artist who just happens to use public walls as his canvas. Who is he? Banksy, of course. Whoever he is, he can certainly be amusing: one of his most popular pieces was in the penguin enclosure at London Zoo, where he spray-painted 'We're bored of fish' in 7-foot-high letters. Banksy is also a British success story: he graduated from graffiti artist to filmmaker when his fascinating documentary *Exit Through the Gift Shop* was released today in 2010. It went on to be nominated for an Oscar. Who would have thought it?

GOLF BANNED!

Golf was invented by the Scots, who wanted a game that would be more fun when played on a hilly pitch with wildlife wandering around (bunkers were originally shelters scraped by sheep in sandy soil). But it proved *too* popular: on this day in 1457, King James II of Scotland issued a law banning 'ye golf' (and football) because his soldiers were having so much fun swinging their niblicks around that they were neglecting their archery practice.

ROCK OF AGES

James Hutton was one day examining Edinburgh's rocky environs when he came to the conclusion that land was eroded by air and water and deposited as layers in the sea, where heat and pressure then consolidated the sediment into stone, and uplifted it into new lands. And so, just like that, he invented modern geology.

Hutton was not only a brilliant Brit, but also a modest one; he waited 25 years to publish his findings (today in 1785) because, according to a contemporary, 'he was one of those who are much more delighted with the contemplation of truth, than with the praise of having discovered it'.

DON'T PANIC

The Hitchhiker's Guide to the Galaxy, by Douglas Adams, is both uniquely British and yet internationally loved. Its cosmic brand of lunacy, pan-galactic gargleblasters and towels, first graced this galaxy's airwaves today in 1978, and proved so popular it went on to become a series of books ('a trilogy in five parts', Adams wonderfully called it), a TV show, a blockbuster film and another radio series. Chances are we'll all still be raving about it when we are flying around in future spacecrafts of our own.

LONDON EYE OPENS

At 443 feet (135 metres) tall, the London Eye was the largest Ferris wheel in the world when it opened today in 2000. This unmistakable and much-loved landmark has 32 passenger pods (33 really, but pod 13 is always empty), representing London's 32 boroughs. Every year, nearly 4 million people step aboard to enjoy a pigeon-eye view of the capital.

ECONOMIC WITH THE TRUTH

Scotsman Adam Smith's *The Wealth of Nations* is one of the most influential books on economics ever published, and it went on sale today in 1776. The work argues that free market economies are the most productive and beneficial to their societies. It was a huge influence on financial thinkers, governments, philosophers and authors worldwide, and earned Smith the reputation of 'the father of capitalism'. Not quite as nice as being known as Father Christmas, but still quite an accolade.

STREET OF SHAME

No newspapers are actually published in Fleet Street any more, but the name lives on as a general term for the industry. There had been book and legal publishers in the area since the early 16th century. Then, today in 1702, Edward Mallet published the *Daily Courant*, London's first daily newspaper, from premises above the White Hart Inn, establishing the rag trade for which the street would eventually become internationally famous.

HOLY MOTHERS

12 The Church of England may have had a woman as its Supreme Governor for 40 years, but below her it was male priests all the way down until today in 1994, when the Church finally took the progressive (and to some, controversial) step of ordaining its first women priests. According to a recent report, by the year 2025 there will be as many female priests as men. Currently, there are around 2,200 female priests and just under 4,500 male priests.

GROW UP AND BE COUNTED

13 Before this day in 1970, if you were a 20-year-old Briton, you could fight for your country, pay taxes, drink alcohol *and* get married – but not vote. Which seems a little unfair considering you could die for your country in battle but not be counted in an election. But then, Britain was one of the first countries in the world to lower the voting age to the now-established 18. In Uzbekistan, for example, you still have to be over 25 to cast your ballot to get your voice heard.

THIS IS GROUND CONTROL

The Jodrell Bank observatory in Cheshire has achieved many notable world firsts. Its Transit Telescope was the largest radio telescope in the world when built, and the Lovell Telescope was the largest steerable dish radio telescope in the world, at a mighty 250 feet in diameter. Lovell's vast motor system reused the gun turret mechanisms from the battleships HMS *Revenge* and *Royal Sovereign*. But the observatory really made its mark on the world today in 1960 when it set a new record by establishing contact with the American Pioneer V satellite at a distance of 407,000 miles.

WHAT'S NEW, PUSSYCAT?

The Reflecting Roadstud was invented by Yorkshireman Percy Shaw, who was inspired by the way a cat's eyes (invented millions of years ago by Mother Nature) reflect light in the dark. His company (opened for business today in 1935) produced millions of them during WWII when abrupt blackouts highlighted their value. Percy also later finessed his invention by adding a rainwater reservoir to the stud's base, making the glass eyes 'self-wiping' when a car drove over them.

POWER TO THE PEOPLE

With its distinctive four leg-like chimneys, Battersea Power Station has to be one of the world's strangest landmarks. Building started today in 1929, and the station was completed in two identical halves, twenty years apart. Despite now being little more than a shell it is still the largest brick building in Europe. It has also, thanks in part to 70s rock band Pink Floyd – gone on to become an eerie, yet iconic, visual landmark along the River Thames.

WOULD YOU ADAM AND EVE IT

Building the world's largest greenhouse in an old clay pit might seem a bit bonkers, but Tim Smit was a man with a vision. His Eden Project in Cornwall took 2½ years to construct but was a runaway success when it opened today in 2001, with a million people visiting every year. Its two biomes re-create rainforest and Mediterranean environments and contain 100,000 plant species from all around the world.

SIGN OF THE TIMES

British Sign Language isn't just a manual version of English, it is its own official language, equivalent to Welsh or Gaelic, and was recognised as such today in 2003. Try to use your British sign skills in America and you will not be understood: their signing is closer to how they do it in France. Which can get quite confusing, I imagine.

MARTYRS TO A GOOD CAUSE

When six farm labourers from Tolpuddle, Dorset, were sentenced to transportation (i.e. deported to Australia) today in 1834, they can hardly have guessed they would be helping create the trade union movement. The Tolpuddle Martyrs simply wanted to protect their wages in the face of the rising mechanisation of farming. But they became popular heroes – 800,000 signatures were collected for their release and their supporters organised one of the first successful demonstration marches in the UK. All were eventually released.

PC PICKLES

20 Britain is famous for its brilliant fictional detectives, but when the coveted Jules Rimet trophy, on display in Britain for the upcoming World Cup finals, was stolen today in 1966, the world hoped we could find a real one just as perceptive. No problem, old boy – up stepped Pickles, a black and white collie. This noble hound was out being walked by his owner David Corbett today in South London when he sniffed an interesting parcel jammed under a hedge. Encouraging David to untie the parcel's string, Pickles was pleased to see that he had just sniffed out the stolen golden trophy. England went on to win the tournament for the first and only time. Pickles, sadly, died choking on his lead while chasing a cat.

LOOK, NO HANDS

21 Today in 1963 saw the introduction of a whole new generation of computer-controlled trains to the London Underground. These technological marvels didn't need a driver to start, accelerate or brake, although they still require an operator on board for safety reasons and to bellow 'Mind the gap!' repetitively at each and every station.

SCANDALISED

Here in Britain, we like to do things properly – especially when it comes to sex scandals. And today in 1963, the greatest gaffe of the lot occurred when the Secretary of State for War, John Profumo, denied any impropriety with the model Christine Keeler. Of course, Profumo *had* been up to all sorts of naughty mischief, which was nearly a disaster for us all because Christine was also linked romantically to a naval attaché at the Soviet Embassy. Profumo later resigned and the affair, along with both their careers, went down in infamy.

A VOTE FOR PROGRESS

This day in 1832 saw an important step on the journey towards modern democracy, with the passing of the 'Great Reform Act'. Corruption in the British electoral system was rife (and getting worse), with 'rotten boroughs' putting seats in landlords' pockets (the Duke of Norfolk controlled *eleven* constituencies). The new Act swept much of the rot away, giving fairer representation to larger populations and increased the electorate (those actually eligible to vote) from 400,000 to 650,000.

TIME TO SET SAIL

24 Determining longitude (how far east or west you were) was a thorny problem in the 18th century. Navigation errors led to many shipwrecks so, since sea trade was becoming the key to world power, Parliament offered £20,000 (£2.87 million in today's money) as a prize for measuring longitude. Then clockmaker John Harrison (born today in 1693) invented the marine chronometer, a timepiece accurate to within seconds on a trans-Atlantic voyage. It revolutionised navigation, helping fellow Brit James Cook steer his way to Australia and Hawaii and ushering in a new era of ocean exploration.

THE GOOD CAPTAIN

25 Captain Thomas Coram was a shipbuilder and merchant who became dismayed at the number of abandoned babies he saw in London. So he set up one of the world's first official charities, the Foundling Hospital, which took in its first children today in 1741. The original hospital in central London was demolished in the 1920s, but its site has since been turned into a children's play area, known as Coram's Fields.

BLAZING GOOD FUN

Fans of bright blazers and outrageously loud ties can take heart that the great Royal Regatta of Henley was founded today in 1839. The event, a *very* British affair and now an important date in the social calendar, was first organised by Captain Edmund Gardiner after seeing how popular the Oxford–Cambridge race had become. So, Gardiner proposed an annual regatta to 'be a source of amusement and gratification to the neighbourhood, and the public in general'. If only Gardiner knew how culturally significant it would eventually become?

WRAPPED AROUND HIS LITTLE FINGER

Shoelaces, as well as other various forms of attaching shoe to foot, had been stopping people's shoes falling off for centuries, but Englishman Harvey Kennedy's flash of inspiration was to physically patent the invention – basically two strings of leather – which he did today in 1790. Suffice to say, he made shoeloads of cash by doing so.

YOU REAP WHAT YOU SOW

28 Jethro Tull, we salute you. No, not the band, although they are a British institution too. The original Jethro Tull (baptised today in 1674) was a British agricultural pioneer who perfected a horse-drawn seed drill. Before Tull, seeds were broadcast by hand, a very inefficient and slow process. Tull's 1701 invention sowed the seeds in neat rows, raising production by as much as 800 per cent and helped to kickstart the Agricultural Revolution.

LIVE FROM KENSINGTON

29 The Royal Albert Hall is one of the most recognisable buildings in the UK and it was first opened by Queen Victoria today in 1871. The world's top performers in all artistic fields have graced its famous stage, from the Proms to Pink Floyd, Sumo wrestlers to school orchestras. It was so vast and impressive when built that unfortunately it had a noticeable echo. This was solved in 1969 with the installation of several large sound-diffusing mushrooms on the ceiling. Just look up and you'll see them.

GAW' BLESS YOU, MUM

Today in 2002 was a sad day for us Brits, but also one that sparked a spontaneous outpouring of national pride and remembrance. The nation's favourite great-grandmother, husband of stuttering King George VI and British Institution in her own right, the Queen Mum, died in her sleep at the grand old age of 101. Tributes flooded in from all corners of society for the inspirational lady whose amazing life overlapped with that of Queen Victoria.

F FOR FAST

The McLaren F1 is the supercar that left the rest of the world eating its dust. Designed and built in Britain, it set the record for the fastest road car in the world, clocking a whopping 240 mph today in 1998. With a price tag of £540,000, it was the most expensive car ever built, and as only 106 were ever made, it was also one of the most exclusive too.

APRIL

BOUNCING INTO HISTORY

 Although the modern sport of bungee jumping was popularised in New Zealand, the very first elasticated jumps were made today in 1979 by five lads from the Oxford University Dangerous Sports club, who decided it would be a good idea to tie their feet to a giant rubber band and jump off the 250-foot-high Clifton Suspension Bridge that links Bristol and North Somerset. As it transpired, it was bloody good fun and bunjee jumping soon became the number one must-try adrenaline activity at exotic tourist locations around the world ... as well as the odd car park in Swindon.

RADAR'S FIRST BLIP

In early 1935, the Air Ministry thought Nazi Germany might have a 'death ray' capable of flattening cities using radio waves, so they asked Scottish scientist Robert Watson-Watt (a descendant of inventor James Watt – see 19 January) to investigate. He concluded that the 'death ray' was an impossibility, but suggested that radio waves could be used to locate enemy aircraft. Just a few weeks later, he had a working model of his system and on this very special day Watson-Watt received a patent for what would later become known as RADAR (Radio Detection and Ranging).

PUNK SPITS IN YOUR FACE

Punk rock might not be to everyone's taste, but you can't deny its popularity in Britain. In 1976, London was *the* place to be if you were a phlegm-spitting, safety-pin-wearing, anarchist.

On this day in 1976, the Sex Pistols were supporting rock band The 101ers whose lead singer was so blown away by the Pistols that he decided punk was the future, left his band and quickly formed a new group. He was Joe Strummer, his next band was The Clash, and their punk songs rocked the world ... then spat in its face.

ZEBRA CROSSINGS INTRODUCED

 There were designated pedestrian crossings before this day in 1949, but they were largely ignored by motorists and pedestrians alike. Then Britain brought the unmistakable zebra crossing into the world. There were 1,000 crossings at first, and their stripes were blue and yellow – not very Zebra like.

The world's most famous zebra crossing is the one featured on The Beatles' *Abbey Road* album in North London. It is perhaps the only traffic-safety feature that is also a rock and roll landmark.

EXCISE ACT PASSED

Dozens of countries may produce whisk(e)y, but aficionados worldwide agree there's nothing quite like a Scottish single malt. This drink largely owes its popularity to the Excise Act passed today in 1823, which eased restrictions on licensed distilleries. This gave birth to the modern era of Scotch production, and when the *Phylloxera* bug destroyed France's wine and cognac production in 1880, Scotch whisky became *the* internationally sought-after spirit ... and not much has changed since then.

HARRODS OPENS

Harrods (opened today in 1824) is the ultimate British shop. As well as being a supplier of the finest luxury items required in life (as well as turning everyday necessities into expensive treats), it is also Britain's largest store by quite some distance. It covers five acres (about three football pitches) and has over one million square feet of selling space across 330 separate departments. Shame it's owned by Qatar, really.

IT'S TEA O'CLOCK

If you're one of the millions of Brits who simply can't function before your morning cuppa, say a little 'thank you' this morning to Frank Clarke, a Birmingham gunsmith, who back in 1902 patented his 'Apparatus Whereby a Cup of Tea or Coffee is Automatically Made'. He later marketed this more snappily as 'A Clock That Makes Tea!' and so the first practical teasmade was born. Teasmade are no longer in fashion, but we should start a campaign to bring them back!

BARKING MAD

8 It was way back today in 1891 that Charles Cruft first held his eponymous dog show, and celebrated British day out in the social calendar, at the Royal Agricultural Hall, Islington. On that day, there were 2,437 entries across 36 breeds. Now around 28,000 dogs enter Crufts each year, bringing 160,000 humans with them, making it the world's largest annual dog show (and the highlight of the year for poop-scoop manufacturers).

SUPERSONIC SUPERSTAR

9 Today in 1969, that glorious symbol of British (and French, of course) engineering excellence, the supersonic passenger jet Concorde, made its maiden flight from Filton, Bristol to RAF Fairford, Gloucestershire. Since these places are only 37 miles apart, and the fancy jet could travel faster than the speed of sound, it probably didn't take very long. But still, a great acheivement anyway. Round of applause, please!

APRIL

THE WRITING OF COPYRIGHT

Before this day in 1710, the Stationers' Company (one of the Livery Companies of the City of London) had a monopoly on England's printing trade. All books had to be entered on their register and only a Company member could do so; corruption and censorship were rife. Then the Statute of Anne introduced the world's first copyright legislation. Now publishers had 14 years' legal protection and the author was identified as the legal owner of the work.

STONE OF DESTINY

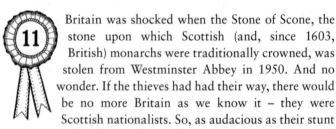

Britain was shocked when the Stone of Scone, the stone upon which Scottish (and, since 1603, British) monarchs were traditionally crowned, was stolen from Westminster Abbey in 1950. And no wonder. If the thieves had had their way, there would be no more Britain as we know it – they were Scottish nationalists. So, as audacious as their stunt was, it's comforting to know that the stone was recovered today, on the site of the altar of Arbroath Abbey, and Britain's future remains safe.

A VITAL BREAKTHROUGH IN TEAPOT TECHNOLOGY

Before William Cookworthy (born today in 1705) came along, tea in Europe was a drink enjoyed only by the upper classes. Porcelain, the preferred material for making teapots, was only made in China, pricing it out of most people's reach. Cookworthy – a sort of Robin Hood figure, but for tea – devised a way of making porcelain in Plymouth, helping everyone rich or poor enjoy a lovely cuppa.

He was also one of the first people to suggest that sailors could avoid scurvy by eating fresh fruit and vegetables.

OFFICER CLASS

Established today in 1741, the Royal Military Academy at Woolwich was the factory for British fighting men with stiff upper lips and a never-say-die attitude. For nearly 200 years, until it closed in 1939, it trained the officers who would go on to shape Britain's massive empire – which at one point had colonised a quarter of the entire planet. However, one of the suprise achievements of the Royal Military Academy was the invention of, somewhat bizarrely, the popular, and very British game of snooker – by a former Academy cadet in India in 1875.

APRIL

MINI MARVELS

14 Small but perfectly formed – that's what made the Mini so beloved when it was launched today in 1959. It came into being because Leonard Lord, head of the British Motor Corporation, was irritated by all the cheap German cars on British roads: 'God damn these bloody awful bubble cars. We must drive them off the road by designing a proper miniature car.' And so he (or rather Alec Issigonis) did.

When three Minis (coloured red, white and blue respectively, of course) appeared as the getaway cars in the classic British film *The Italian Job* in 1969, their iconic status was sealed.

WONDERFUL WANDERING

15 We've all seen a bed of spring daffodils and thought, 'Ooh, they're nice.' But few of us have turned that observation into a major literary movement. In fact, just one of us – William Wordsworth. He was out with his sister today in 1802 when he spotted said yellow flowers and promptly went off and wrote 'I Wandered Lonely as a Cloud'. It became his most famous work, helped to inspire the popularity of English romanticism and remains one of Britain's most-loved poems.

ONE NAMES THIS SHIP *BRITANNIA*

16 Launched today in 1953, the Royal Yacht *Britannia* was the Queen's home-from-home for 44 years. Hundreds of dignitaries around the world enjoyed the hospitality of what was virtually a floating palace, before the ship retired to Leith Docks in Edinburgh. She steamed 1,087,623 nautical miles in her lifetime, making the Queen the most-travelled monarch the world has ever known.

ON YE OLDE ROAD

17 Today in 1397, Geoffrey Chaucer told his *Canterbury Tales* for the first time at the court of Richard II. Chaucer's poetic epic isn't just one of the major early works in English and a world literary classic, it's also the genesis of a genre that pervades today's teenage movies. For the adventures of the motley crew of tale-telling Canterbury pilgrims is surely the world's first road trip – where debauchery, misadventure and hedonism are the key themes.

PRESSED INTO ACTION

Extreme ironing – the danger sport that combines the thrills of a dangerous outdoor activity with the satisfaction that only a well-pressed shirt can accomplish – could *only* have been invented in Britain. Back in 2002, Phil Shaw combined adrenaline sport with tedious housework and thrill (and crease) seekers have been snapped all over the world pressing their smalls on mountain tops, dangling from parachutes and even at the bottom of the ocean. But, today in 2011, extreme ironing (it just sounds ridiculous, doesn't it?) got one of its crowning achievements when drivers heading north on the M1 were astonished to see a man – in his dressing gown, no less – ironing a shirt on the southbound carriageway. Thankfully, the road had been temporarily closed, but to anyone driving by it must have been very funny to see … and I bet the guy in the dressing gown was in creases!

IS ZIT IN IT?

After more than 70 years of scholarship, sweat and tears, today in 1928 saw the publication of the final section of the *Oxford English Dictionary*. It defined 600,000 words, the most of any world dictionary at the time, and extended to 12 volumes. More importantly, Britain's bored schoolboys could finally look up all the rude words beginning with Z.

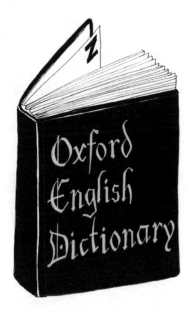

TRIAL BY BATTLE

 British's often quirky laws are world famous, but this one was particularly bonkers. In 1817, Abraham Thornton was charged with the murder of Mary Ashford. He was acquitted, but Mary's brother, William Ashford, appealed and Thornton was rearrested. Thornton then pulled out two leather gauntlets and threw one down in the court, claiming the right to *trial by battle*. The court scratched its collective head, but this was Thornton's right under a medieval law relating to private appeals that had never been repealed, and his request was granted. Since Ashford declined the option of mortal combat, Thornton was freed on this day in 1818. The right to private appeals, and with that the right to trial by battle, was repealed the next year.

SUITS YOU, SIR

On this day in 1846, Henry Poole moved to Savile Row and started a trend for the street to be the international epitome of men's premier quality tailoring. Indeed, the word 'bespoke' originated on the street, from the reference to cloth that was said to 'be spoken for' by individual clientele. Henry Poole also invented the Tuxedo while on Savile Row. Originally made for the Prince of Wales in 1860, an American visitor took one of the classic, tailored suits back to the US and caused a sensation when he wore it at the Tuxedo Club in upstate New York.

To this day, Savile Row is still regarded as a powerhouse of fancy, classy tailoring around the world – even if you don't see as many Tuxedos and top hats as you used to.

I AM SAILING

After 10 months alone at sea in his 32-foot boat *Suhaili*, British yachtsman Sir Robin Knox-Johnston sailed into Falmouth today in 1969 and became the first person to make a solo non-stop circumnavigation of the world.

There were seven other sailors attempting the feat as part of a challenge laid down by the *Sunday Times*, but one by one they all dropped out, leaving Knox-Johnston the only finisher.

ST GEORGE'S DAY

As patron saints go, St George doesn't really inspire much in the way of national celebration, certainly compared with St Patrick. Maybe this is because he was actually a Roman soldier who was born in Syria. Nonetheless, his cross is a fundamental part of the national flag, so today why not go out and chase a dragon or two in his honour? Curiously, St George is also the patron saint of those suffering from syphilis. He certainly deserves a clap for that.

THESE BOOTS ARE MADE FOR WALKING

It's a historic day for those of us who love the great British outdoors – today in 1965, the Pennine Way was formally opened. One of Britain's most challenging long-distance trails, it stretches for 267 glorious miles from Edale in the Peak District, north through the Yorkshire Dales and the Northumberland National Park, to finish at Kirk Yetholm in Scotland.

GET YOURSELF IN THE PICTURE

25 Since it first opened on this day in 1769, The Royal Academy's Summer Exhibition in Piccadilly has shown off the work of some of Britain's greatest artists, including Turner, Gainsborough and Hockney. But the truly wonderful thing is that the exhibition is open to everyone – if you've done a nice picture of your cat using poster paints, you are welcome to enter it. Just pay your £25 fee and send it in.

Go on, you could be the next Constable …

THE MARK OF BRITISH QUALITY

26 When several prominent civil engineers met today in 1901 under the leadership of Sir John Wolfe-Barry (who designed Tower Bridge, London), they wanted to standardise steel sizes for industry. This 'Engineering Standards Committee' was successful, cutting the number of tramway rail gauges from 75 to 5 and saving millions. The committee later became the British Standards Institution and their famous Kitemark® became a stamp of trusted quality recognised worldwide. Have a look at any window or fire exstinguisher in the country and you'll see this famous symbol.

PALACE OF WESTMINSTER STARTED

The site of the Houses of Parliament was originally a royal palace, first established in the 11th century. Kings and queens lived at Westminster until a fire gutted the complex in 1512.

Parliament then took over, but, in 1834, an even greater fire destroyed the buildings. A national competition to design a replacement parliament building was won by Charles Barry's gothic pile. Today in 1840, the foundation stone was laid for the rebuilding of Westminster, the building that would come to symbolise Britain's power, history and heritage more than any other.

BLIGH'S REVENGE

The famous Mutiny on the Bounty, which happened today in 1789, has long been portrayed as Fletcher Christian's courageous uprising against the tyrant William Bligh. But Bligh wasn't so harsh by the standards of the day, and he was one of the most phenomenal sailors Britain has ever produced. Cast adrift in an open boat with no instruments, he navigated 3,618 nautical miles of tumultuous seas to reach safety. The mutineers mostly ended up killing each other.

KATE & WILL TIE THE WINDSOR KNOT

29 Today in 2011, Britain (and much of the rest of the world) came to a halt to watch a fairytale come true. Well, a large number of men promptly took to the golf course, but still the marriage of Prince William to 'commoner' Catherine Middleton was a wonderful occasion that sparked the biggest celebrations of everything British in decades. The country enjoyed a national holiday, street parties (with government-funded bunting) and blanket TV coverage of the entire day – especially Kate's dress. And yes, the new Duchess of Cornwall did look lovely.

HANDY LANDY

30 The Land Rover – a beacon of British car manufacturing – was built to be the toughest thing on four wheels, and was an instant hit with hardy-car lovers when it debuted at the Amsterdam Motor Show today in 1948. British Farmers could plough fields with them, the Army could happily drop them out of planes and explorers could run their 'Landy' for a few thousand miles on banana oil if that's all they had to hand. Sixty years later, around 70 per cent of all Land Rovers ever built are still chugging through the world's bogs, deserts and jungles.

MAY

A TRULY GREAT EXHIBITION

The Great Exhibition of 1851, which was opened today by Queen Victoria, was intended as a magnificent advertisement of Britain's industrial and artistic prowess. It featured exhibits from all over the world, but pride of place was given to home-grown wonders. In its six-month run, 6 million people – equivalent to a third of the entire population of Britain at the time – visited the exhibition. Its £186,000 (£16,190,000 today) profit was used to found the now-world renowned Victoria and Albert Museum, the Science Museum and the Natural History Museum.

HEAVEN'S BELLS

 The glorious sound of church bells ringing out is, for many, the archetypal soundtrack of the English village. Change ringing is the art of ringing a set of church bells in a series of intricate patterns or 'changes'. Accomplishing a full 'peal' of bells – a pattern of a set length that has no repeated changes – is a prodigious feat of concentration and physical effort. The first true peal happened today back in 1715 at the 14-bell church of St Peter Mancroft in Norwich. The ringers went through 5,040 changes of a pattern called 'Plain Bob Triples'.

FESTIVAL OF BRITAIN

The Festival of Britain was a national exhibition that opened in London and around Britain today in 1951. Its aim was to help revive British culture, industry and national spirit after being depleted during World War Two. The principal exhibition site was on the South Bank of the River Thames where a whole new public space was created amid modernist exhibition buildings, including the Royal Festival Hall. There were also installations in other parts of London and the UK, as well as exhibitions that toured Britain by land and sea.

ROYCE MEETS ROLLS

Britain may not produce the same quantity of cars it once did, but we still make some of the best. Charles Rolls and Henry Royce met for the first time today in 1904 at the Midland Hotel in Manchester and agreed to work together with the simple aim of producing the finest motor cars in the world.

Their uncompromising pursuit of quality has attracted a loyal following among the planet's rich and famous. An eclectic mix of Rolls-Royce fans includes General Franco, John Lennon, Brigitte Bardot, Sylvester Stallone, P. Diddy, Alan Sugar and Elvis Presley.

HOSTAGES FREED – LIVE ON TV!

The SAS had existed as a special forces regiment since 1941, but it was their starring role in the Iranian Embassy siege today in 1980 that brought them to the world's attention. Terrorists had seized the embassy on 30 April and had just shot a hostage when the SAS stormed the building live on TV. Abseiling on to balconies from the roof, they used frame charges and stun grenades to blast their way in, before killing five of the six militants and rescuing nineteen hostages.

GILBERT SCOTT FINDS HIS CALLING

The red phone box is a British design classic, but it was actually the sixth attempt at creating a national phone booth. Architect Giles Gilbert Scott – also responsible for Liverpool Cathedral and Battersea Power Station (see 16 March) – won a competition to create the box and his K6 (kiosk number six) design was rolled out today in 1935.

There were 73,000 in Britain by 1980 and, although many have since been replaced, around 2,000 have listed status.

THINKING SMALL

7 Today in 1952, British electronics engineer Geoffrey Dummer presented the first public description of an integrated circuit, or microchip as it became later popularised. His conceptual breakthrough was to visualise electronic equipment as a solid block of conducting material with no connecting wires. Components could then be smaller and more reliable, marking a giant step towards modern personal computers.

TURNING THE TIDE

8 London has always been vulnerable to flooding, but 1953's huge North Sea storm focused the minds of the powers that be. After years of study and discussion, the Thames Barrier was finally opened today in 1984. This engineering marvel is raised when a predicted storm surge combines with unfavourable tides and river flow, preventing the flood waters inundating the capital. Those who doubt climate change is happening may like to note that the barrier was raised 4 times in the 1980s, 35 times in the 1990s and 75 times in the 2000s...

RIDDLE OF THE ENIGMA

9 On this day in 1941, the German submarine *U-110* was captured after the Royal Navy damaged her with depth charges. That was an impressive achievement, but on board was a prize that really made this a day to remember. As one of the boarding sailors, William Pollock, was investigating the radio room, he spotted a portable device that looked out of place and took it. This turned out to be one of the latest Enigma cryptography machines. Allied cryptographers later used it to crack German codes and by doing so shortened World War II by a predicted two years.

ART FOR ALL

10 Britain's National Gallery isn't the world's biggest (that's the State Hermitage museum in Russia) but it is splendid and, importantly, free to enter since it first opened today in 1824. Originally opened in a townhouse at No. 100 Pall Mall with just 38 paintings, this soon became far too small as the collection grew, and in 1832 construction began on a landmark building in the then-new Trafalgar Square. To this day it is still one of London's top draws for tourists.

LOTSA LOOS

11 A statue of the 1966 World Cup-winning captain Bobby Moore was unveiled today in 2007, marking the opening of the new and improved Wembley stadium. This magnificent (and massive) stadium is not just the most capacious in Britain (90,000) and one of the largest in the world; it also boasts the most lavatories of any venue anywhere – 2,618, to be exact.

PLASTIC FANTASTIC

12 Today in 1862, Birmingham inventor Alexander Parkes displayed the world's first plastic at the 1862 London International Exhibition. He modestly called it Parkesine (well you would, wouldn't you?), but it would later be developed as celluloid. Parkes' plastic enabled photographs to be produced on a flexible material (rather than glass or metal), effectively making motion pictures possible.

MAGNIFICENT MEN IN THEIR FLYING MACHINES

The Wright brothers only made their first powered flight in 1903, but within a few years it was clear that flying aircraft had huge military potential. And today in 1912 the Royal Flying Corps (which later became the Royal Air Force) was established. At first, the Corps only had 12 manned balloons and 36 aeroplanes. These days it has over 1000 aircraft and around 45,000 personnel.

JENNER JOUSTS WITH SMALLPOX

In 1796, smallpox killed around 400,000 people a year in Europe alone. Then British scientist Edward Jenner learned that milkmaids who caught the cowpox virus (a similar, less virulent disease) did not catch smallpox. Today, he inoculated his gardener's eight-year-old son with material from the cowpox blisters of the hand of a milkmaid and in doing so created the world's first vaccine.

In 1979, thanks to mass vaccination, smallpox was declared eradicated worldwide – Jenner's ingenious discovery has probably saved more lives than any other.

SQUARE SHOT IN A ROUND HOLE

15 The Puckle gun, patented today in 1718 by English inventor James Puckle, was the world's first machine gun. That's not a very nice thing to boast about, but the invention itself was madly eccentric: it could fire round shot at 'civilised' enemies and square shot at Turks. Puckle reasoned that, since the square shot caused more damage, this would convince the Turks of the benefits of our Christian 'civilisation'.

BOSWELL FINDS HIS JOHNSON

16 Today in 1763, two very different Britons met for the first time: Samuel Johnson and James Boswell. Johnson was established as England's foremost man of letters, a brilliant poet, critic and lexicographer; Boswell was a young Scot (whom Johnson originally disliked), a second-rate advocate and heavy drinker. But this original 'odd couple' enjoyed a remarkable and historic friendship. Boswell found the inspiration for his *Life of Johnson* (often regarded as the finest biography ever written), and Johnson enjoyed the company a loyal and witty companion who seemed to truly understand his eccentricities.

ROYAL NAVY FOUNDED

From the 17th century until well into the 20th century, the Royal Navy was the most powerful sea force in the world, powering Britain's colonial expansion and protecting her burgeoning trade. The organisation of the Royal Navy was one of the contributing factors to its world dominance for three centuries. It took much of its modern form today in 1661 when the Naval Discipline Act (co-written by diarist Samuel Pepys) was passed.

BEST EVER MOUSETRAP INVENTED

No, we didn't invent the cat. But James Henry Atkinson did invent the Little Nipper Mousetrap (trademarked today in 1909). This murderous machine is a design classic. Made of wood and wire, it is cheap and very effective – it slams shut in just 0.038 of a second, faster than any other trap.

The Patent Office holds designs for over 4,400 mousetraps, but the Little Nipper still dispatches around 60 per cent of the world's trapped mice to the great cheese cupboard in the sky.

THESE GO UP TO 11 …

19 In the early 1960s Jim Marshall was running a drum shop when he started importing guitars and amps. His customers (who happened to include Eric Clapton, Jimi Hendrix and Pete Townshend) wanted a louder, more rocking sound, so he founded Marshall Amplification today in 1964. His first masterstroke was the revolutionary JTM45 50-watt amp. When the musicians demanded even *more* oomph, Jim piled up the amplifiers on top of each other, creating the famous speaker stack. This tower of power became must-have stage equipment for all hard-rocking stars and Marshall are still one of the most popular and iconic brands of amplifier in the world.

PROPER PEARLIES

20 The first Pearly King was Henry Croft, a Victorian rat catcher. London's costermongers then wore suits decorated with pearl buttons on the seams. Henry went one step further and completely covered a suit in pearls, including top hat and tails. He became famous and used his celebrity to raise money for charity. His colourful look and voluntary work is continued by the 'Pearlies' who today hold their Memorial Service in Trafalgar Square.

CANAL DREAMS

In the late 19th century, the high dues charged by the Port of Liverpool led developers to plan a large canal reaching from the sea right into the heart of the industrial powerhouse of Manchester. After six years of construction, the Manchester Ship Canal was opened by Queen Victoria today in 1894. This 36-mile engineering marvel was then the world's largest navigation canal. It still carries about 6 million tons of freight each year.

WEAVING WONDERS

Before John Kay patented his flying shuttle today in 1733, weavers could only produce cloth as wide as their arms, since they had to pass the shuttle that held the thread from hand to hand. But Kay's ingenious invention was wheeled and pointed, allowing weavers to shoot it faster across a much wider bed of fabric.

Weaving became hugely more efficient and, more importantly, profitable, helping to drive the Industrial Revolution in a booming Britain.

IRISH 'AYES' ARE SMILING

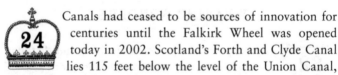

23 After so many years of trouble and conflict in Northern Ireland, today in 1998 brought a bright ray of hope to all parties. In a referendum, 71% of voters from Northern Ireland and 94% in the Irish Republic supported the Good Friday peace agreement. It laid the foundation for devolution and, hopefully, happier times for Britain and Northern Ireland.

BOAT BRILLIANCE

24 Canals had ceased to be sources of innovation for centuries until the Falkirk Wheel was opened today in 2002. Scotland's Forth and Clyde Canal lies 115 feet below the level of the Union Canal, and boats had been unable to move between the two waterways since 1933 when a flight of 11 locks was dismantled.

To restore the connection and capture the world's imagination, British Waterways commissioned the world's first and only rotating boat lift. This beautiful structure is so perfectly balanced that its two 55-ton gondolas can raise 330 tons of water – and a boat – in under five minutes, using only enough electricity to power eight kettles.

ROYAL SEAL OF APPROVAL

25 Having a Royal Warrant above your shop door is a sure sign of quality, and some of the best British manufacturers display them. Henry II gave the first Royal Charter to the Weavers' Company in 1155, and the practice flourished, particularly in Victorian times. Today in 1840, the Royal Tradesmen's Association was formed to help promote the 'best of the best' and there are now around 850 Royal Warrant holders, ranging from Aston Martin to Tom Smith's Christmas crackers.

DEEPEST BLUE

26 Almost nothing was known about the ocean deeps until the landmark study carried out by British scientists aboard HMS *Challenger*, which finished today in 1876. This ship was converted into a floating laboratory for its epic four-year voyage of 68,890 nautical miles. The scientists took thousands of measurements and samples, discovered more than 4,700 new species and laid the foundation for the entire discipline of oceanography. They also first sounded the deepest part of the world's oceans, paying out 4,475 fathoms (26,850 feet) of line before touching bottom in the area now known as the Challenger Deep.

CHELSEA FLOWER SHOW

27 Officially, it is known as the Great Spring Show, but to most British garden fans it is simply the Chelsea Flower Show, the most famous horticultural event in the world. First held today in 1862, it gives gardeners the chance to catch the latest plant trends in what is a virtual catwalk for the gardening world. It is also simply a very beautiful day out and every year 157,000 visitors from many different countries come to check out the tulips.

OPEN-HOUSE OPERA

28 Glyndebourne festival is an English institution. Family-run and financially independent the festival runs annually and is like no other on Earth – think Glastonbury but for toffs instead of commoners. It's *the* music festival, and date in your social calendar, to be seen at, where opera and classical music fit the bill. Well-heeled music lovers in fancy evening dress have flocked to enjoy classical sounds at this country-pad/opera house since the first festival opened today in 1934 with a performance of *Le Nozze di Figaro*.

THE TIME MACHINE ARRIVES IN THE PRESENT

H.G. Wells was one of the few writers influential enough to create an entire genre. His first novel, *The Time Machine*, was published in Britain today in 1895, and he went on to write many more sci-fi classics, including *The Island of Doctor Moreau*, *The Invisible Man*, *The War of the Worlds* and *The First Men in the Moon*.

Before writing professionally, Wells was a teacher. One of his pupils was A.A. Milne, future creator of beloved children's classic *Winnie the Pooh*.

MAKING MONEY IS CHILD'S PLAY

Frank Hornby was a Liverpool bookkeeper who in his spare time made mechanical toys for his sons with pieces cut out from sheet metal. After scrabbling together some money, he marketed the little engineering kits he made, founding Meccano Ltd on this day in 1908, eventually making him a rich man. And he wasn't finished inventing classic British toys – for an encore he created Dinky Toys and gave his name to the national treasure that is the Hornby model railway system.

HEATHROW AIRPORT TAKES OFF

31 Heathrow Airport (which opened today in 1946) may be the world's busiest international airport, but we all know the airport itself is nothing to be proud of. And yet maybe that's the point: it shows a certain confidence in the rest of our country's wonders and attractions that we're prepared to let visitors' first impression of Britain be a cramped concrete-warren of lost luggage, oleaginous burger joints, chaotic baggage reclaim carousels and endless, countless, queues full of exhausted and despairing travellers who just want to be *anywhere* else but there. Welcome to Britain!

JUNE

A MAGNETIC PERSONALITY

It's hard enough finding the North Magnetic Pole nowadays – the pesky thing moves 35 miles a year. Back in 1831, it took a very intrepid gentleman by the name of James Clark Ross to pin it down on this day as it meandered across the wastes of northern Canada. Ross was a truly great British explorer whose name is attached to a rather large area of the world: the Ross Sea in Antarctica is named after him, as is the Ross Ice Shelf and Ross Island.

QUEEN ELIZABETH II'S CORONATION, 1953

Queen Elizabeth II isn't just the British monarch, she is also the Supreme Governor of the Church of England, Queen of 16 independent sovereign states, the figurehead of the 54-member Commonwealth of Nations and the patron of over 600 charities and other organisations. How she finds the time to walk her corgis I don't know, but today in 1953, at the age of just 25, she became our Queen. God bless her.

IT LIVES ...

The blood-curdling tale of the monster created from spare body parts and galvanised into life by Victor Frankenstein is one of the most haunting and influential stories of all time. Even more remarkable is the fact that *Frankenstein; or, The Modern Prometheus* was written by an 18-year-old girl, Mary Shelley. She spent the wet summer of 1816 with the poet Percy Shelley and Lord Byron, each writing stories for the others' amusement. Mary picked up her pen and gave life to a monster ... and a legend. In the book Frankenstein's monster is never given a name, though Shelley herself did refer to it as ... Adam.

RALEIGH REALLY IN A HURRY

4 Sir Walter Raleigh epitomised the British hero who jolly well just got on with things. He founded the first English colony in North Carolina today in 1584, mounted not one but *two* expeditions to find the fabled city of El Dorado, and popularised tobacco in England. Raleigh also commissioned the first *Ark Royal* and planted the first potatoes in Ireland. As he was summoned to the executioner's block for conspiring against King James I, his last words as he lay his head down were: 'Strike, man! Strike!' Stiff upper lip or what!

MARKS & SPARKS

5 Despite a recent financial, and public, wobble, Marks & Spencer is still one of Britain's most beloved shops. It was founded in 1884 when Michael Marks, from Poland, and Thomas Spencer, a cashier from Yorkshire, set up a stall in Kirkgate Market, Leeds. Until 2002, Marks & Spencer *only* sold British-made goods and its 'St Michael' brand (introduced today in 1928) was a symbol of fine quality and value for money.

D-DAY

Operation Overlord was the invasion of German-held Western Europe by British and Allied forces, which started today in 1944 with D-Day. More than 155,000 troops crossed the English Channel to the Normandy beaches in the largest amphibious military operation in history. Its success led to the liberation of Paris on 25 August and the eventual withdrawal of German forces.

DEDICATED FORERUNNER OF FASHION

Beau Brummell (born today in 1778) was a famous dandy of Regency England who established the gentlemen's fashion of tailored dark suits with full-length trousers worn with a cravat. He claimed it took him five hours to dress and that he polished his boots with champagne. That might sound ridiculous but it's thanks to him that people all over the world wear a suit with a tie. Beau established and championed this good-looking combination and it soon became *the* fashion of the day. Way to go, Beau.

WEDGWOOD SERVED UP TO ROYALTY

8 Josiah Wedgwood was an unlikely candidate to be the 'Father of English Potters'. Smallpox left him with a bad leg that was later amputated, making it impossible for him to even turn a potter's wheel. But when he perfected an elegant cream-coloured earthenware, it earned royal approval (today in 1766) and this 'Queen's Ware' established his fame, which grew rapidly. So too did his fortune, thanks to his extraordinary marketing nous: direct mail, money-back guarantees, the travelling salesmen, self-service, free delivery, buy one get one free, illustrated catalogues; they *all* came from Josiah Wedgwood.

TOP OF ALL CLASSES

9 Bertrand Russell was one of the most brilliant academics of the 20th century and one of those rare polymaths who accomplish feats of genius in several disciplines. Philosopher, mathematician and historian, he received the Order of Merit today in 1949 and won the Nobel Prize for Literature in 1950. He is also the only Welshman with a street named after him in Amsterdam.

RACING INTO HISTORY

10 The first University Boat Race took place on this day in 1829 at Henley-on-Thames, before later moving to Putney. The Boat Race is one of the most famous sporting events in the world, with millions watching every year on TV and around 250,000 people lining the riverbank.

It's also a notoriously tough race, being held no matter how nasty the conditions. Cambridge sank in 1859 and 1978, Oxford in 1925 and 1951, and both boats went down in 1912.

YOU DON'T HAVE TO PRONOUNCE IT TO ENJOY IT

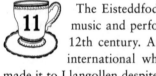

11 The Eisteddfod is a Welsh festival of literature, music and performance, which dates back to the 12th century. And, on this day in 1947, it went international when 40 choirs from 14 countries made it to Llangollen despite a rail strike. It has since become one of the world's great music festivals, with Luciano Pavarotti, Kiri Te Kanawa, Yehudi Menuhin, Bryn Terfel and Katherine Jenkins just some of the famous names who have made their mark here.

ALL THE WORLD'S A STAGE

12 It took 27 years of planning and four of construction, but the replica of Shakespeare's Globe theatre on the South Bank finally opened today in 1997 with a performance of *Henry V*. It's as close to the original circular playhouse as possible: made of English oak, it has a thrust stage, three tiers of steep seating, space for 700 'groundlings' and the first and only thatched roof permitted in London since the Great Fire of 1666.

LOVE/HATE RELATIONSHIP

13 There are different versions of Marmite around the world, but only the British one makes the roof of your mouth feel like you've just snorted gunpowder. If you're a fan of that feeling, then you ought to know that The Marmite Food Extract Company was formed today in 1902 in Burton upon Trent. This famous brewing town was chosen because concocting the yeasty spread demands beer-making by-products. Incidentally, Marmite isn't only good for spreading on toast – in the 1930s, English scientist Lucy Wills used it to identify the beneficial effects of folic acid.

HERE'S LISTENING TO YOU, KID ...

14 In early 1931, electrical engineer Alan Blumlein went to see a film with his wife. Cinemas then only had a single set of speakers, and Blumlein thought it unacceptable that the actor's voice came from the left when his face was on the right-hand side of the screen. He told his wife that he would fix that problem and promptly went back to his lab and invented stereo sound, which he patented on this day of that same year.

RIGHTS ARE WRITTEN

15 On this day in 1215, King John attached his Great Seal to the Magna Carta at Runnymede. This historic document started as a cunning ploy by ambitious barons to weaken the King, but it also gave Britons some important rights. Several are still on the statute books today, including the very important idea that no 'freeman' can be punished except following a trial by his peers.

The Magna Carta also influenced the constitutions of many other countries, including the United States.

JAM, JERUSALEM & JEZEBELS

16 When the British Women's Institute was founded today in 1915, it had two clear goals: to revitalise rural communities and to get women interested in producing food at home during World War One. The third, more glamorous, activity of taking your clothes off for risqué charity calendars was happily adopted in 1999. They even made a film about it – *Calendar Girls* – in 2003

FATHER OF CHEAP ENERGY

The fuel cell in modern hybrid cars might just be the brilliant invention that helps save us when the oil runs out – and it was invented by a Brit, William Grove, on this day in 1842.

Electric cells were all the rage in the science world then, and Grove's bright spark was to grasp that, just as an electric current will split water into its component parts of hydrogen and oxygen, so the reaction could be reversed. By combining hydrogen and oxygen, he produced energy and water without combustion.

NOT ON YOUR LIFE

The first life insurance policy as we know it was taken out today in 1583 by a salter named William Gibbons. It is notable because, even then, the underwriters tried to wriggle out of paying. The term was 12 months and Gibbons duly expired within that period on 29 May 1584. But his heirs were astonished to hear the underwriters claim that 'month' meant a period of 28 days, and so the policy had expired. It went all the way to court before Mr Gibbons was favoured.

BOBBIES ON THE BEAT

19 Before this day in 1829, law and order in London was maintained by volunteer constables and watchmen. As the Industrial Revolution drove exponential growth of the capital, this part-time force became ineffective at crime-fighting. So, Home Secretary Sir Robert Peel recommended a new style of police force: an official, paid profession, organised in a civilian rather than military way. Crucially, it should also be answerable to the public. And so the world's first modern police force was born.

VICTORIA REIGNS SUPREME

20 When Queen Victoria succeeded to the throne today in 1837, it was one of the most significant moments in British history. Just 18 when crowned, she became a national icon, reigning for 63 years and 7 months, longer than any other British monarch and the longest reign of any female monarch in history. The Victorian era saw a flourishing of British industry, culture and science, as well as the expansion of the British Empire which eventually covered around a quarter of the planet.

WHAT'S THIS RIVER DOING HERE?

21 Before all this new-fangled GPS technology, we relied on Ordnance Survey maps to get us lost in the middle of Dartmoor. And the historic map-making experts have been helping Britons mislay perfectly good paths since this day in 1791. The government, wary of invasion from revolutionary France, instructed the Board of Ordnance to accurately survey the south coast. Having successfully mapped Kent at one-inch-to-the-mile by 1801, the OS went on to map the whole country, which took more than twenty years.

HOWZAT!

22 Lord's (named after its founder, Thomas Lord) is the spiritual home of cricket. The ground hosted its first match today in 1814, between Marylebone Cricket Club and Hertfordshire. Lord's also has the world's oldest sporting museum, which contains hundreds of years of celebrated cricket memorabilia, including the Ashes urn. The actual pitch is also remarkable because it has a significant slope: the northwest side of the ground is eight feet higher than the southeast side.

CLIVE'S CRUCIAL WIN

23 Boasting about the extent of the British Empire might be a little un-PC these days, but there's no denying that it was pretty impressive. And today in 1757 marks the day when our forebears really started to get seriously colonial. Robert Clive led a force of the British East India Company in a decisive victory over the Nawab of Bengal and his French allies at the Battle of Plassey. This made the Company the number-one power in South Asia and helped Britain expand its influence over the subcontinent.

OLD, OLD BOYS NETWORK

24 When it comes to distinguished former pupils, Eton is in a class of its own. The archetypal English public school (which first opened its doors today in 1440) has educated a prodigious 19 out of Britain's 47 prime ministers (including David Cameron) and other high-achieving students include George Orwell, Francis Bacon and Ian Fleming.

As you might expect, such a top-flight education doesn't come cheap – it currently costs £29,862 a year to attend Eton.

BASEBALL IS KIDS' STUFF

25 John Newbery was a British publisher who saw that children's books could be both entertaining and educational. His *A Little Pretty Pocket-Book* (published today in 1744) had rhymes for each letter of the alphabet as well as woodcut illustrations. The book seems simple today, but it was nothing short of revolutionary then and became very popular. It also contains the first printed reference to 'baseball'.

GENETICALLY CODIFIED

26 Today in 2000, scientists from the Sanger Centre in London handed over the decoded human genome to the world. They had unravelled 85% of the 3 billion DNA base pairs – the blueprint for every aspect of your body, from the capillaries in your lungs to the colour of your eyes – effectively all the ingredients that makes you *you*. The Human Genome Project could benefit every human on Earth and many believe it is modern science's greatest achievement.

HARRY IS FINGERED

When Harry Jackson stole a set of billiard balls today in 1902, he could hardly have thought that he would go down in history, or that his subsequent prosecution and sentencing to seven years in prison would change the face of worldwide crime detection forever, but that's what happened.

Jackson made the mistake of stealing the balls from a house that had just been painted, so leaving a fingerprint on a windowsill, just as Scotland Yard was perfecting its fingerprint detection procedures.

COMPUTER SAYS YES

Some people are so far ahead of their time it's scary. Charles Babbage was born in 1791, but he had the foresight to invent the first practical computer – the Difference Engine. This mechanical number-cruncher would have been 11 feet long, had 8,000 moving parts and weighed 5 tons – if only Victorian engineers had been able to follow his advanced designs. It wasn't until the Science Museum built a replica and turned it on today in 1991 that they discovered it worked perfectly. It could even print its results!

GONE BUT NOT FORGOTTEN

29 Diana, Princess of Wales (or the people's princess as she was affectionately called) was certainly beloved by all British people, as the spontaneous national outpouring of grief at her untimely death in 1997 showed. Today in 2001 marked a fitting response to that national sentiment, when the Hyde Park water memorial in her honour was dedicated.

THE MAGIC BEGINS

30 Harry Potter has thrilled a whole generation of children (and several generations of adults) since he first appeared today in 1997. *Harry Potter and the Philosopher's Stone* was the first novel in the seven-book series and at first even the publishers only had modest hopes for the tale: they only printed 500 copies and author J.K. Rowling's advance was just £2,500. But kids loved it: within two years, the book was topping bestseller lists worldwide with estimates of book sales well into the hundreds of millions. A new popular legend had been created – one that children will be reading about for many generations to come.

JULY

LANDMARK LEGISLATION

Before this day in 1948, the owner of a building could knock it down if they fancied, and the country lost hundreds of historic structures to the whims of overzealous developers. Then the Town and Country Planning Act was passed, requiring planning permission for new buildings and giving local authorities the power to preserve woodland or buildings of architectural or historic interest.

It was an added hurdle for developers, but a blessing for those of us who love beautiful buildings. There are now more than 500,000 listed buildings in the UK.

GORDON BENNETT!

British Racing Green is one of the most distinctive liveries in world sport, and it was first adopted today in 1903 at the Gordon Bennett Cup, the precursor of Grand Prix races. Ironically, it was chosen in deference to Ireland, which was hosting the event, and was then part of the United Kingdom.

ONE CHANNEL AND NOT MUCH ON

A cynic might contend that the very first image seen on TV set the tone for the vast majority of subsequent programming: it was the head of a ventriloquist's dummy.

But for John Logie Baird, the gadget's Scottish inventor, it was a major breakthrough. After transmitting the first TV picture in 1925, he went on to make long-distance transmissions in 1927 and invent colour TV, which he demonstrated today in 1928. Home entertainment would never be the same again. The world would never be the same again.

LIGHT WHERE YOU LIKE IT

The Anglepoise lamp is still the epitome of the light that is both extremely practical and very stylish, and it was patented today in 1932 by British designer George Carwardine. He was actually a car designer and at the time was specialising in vehicle suspension systems – which is where his idea for the Anglepoise's jointed, spring-tensioned design came from.

STREAKING TAKES OFF, 1799

On a normal 18th-century Friday evening in the City of London, a man was arrested as he ran from Cornhill to Cheapside. He was rather out of breath and utterly naked. When asked why by the bewildered constables, he cheerfully admitted it was for a wager of 10 guineas (£735 today). And so the modern sensation of streaking was born. In its birthday suit, obviously.

JOHN, THIS IS PAUL

6 It was a typical summer fête in England in 1957 – there were Scouts and Guides on decorated floats, Morris dancers and the crowning of the Rose Queen. A young band called The Quarrymen played some skiffle songs in a field behind the church. As the local police dog display team followed them on to the stage, the band's 16-year-old lead singer, John Lennon, went into the Scout hut. A friend introduced him to 15-year-old Paul McCartney, who played John a couple of tunes on his guitar. A few weeks later, Paul joined the band and world music got a shot in the arm it would never recover from. Indeed, culture, society and the world at large woke up to a new sound. The Beatles (as they would later call themselves)would go on to sell one and half *billion* records and be one of the most popular, and influential, groups of all time. And it would never have happened without the events that happened on this day.

THE NOVEL NOW DEPARTING FROM PLATFORM 4 ...

The world doesn't have many train stations named after novels – in fact, only one. *Waverley* by Sir Walter Scott was first published today in 1814 and was phenomenally popular with critics and the public, selling out its first print run of 1,000 copies within two days. It practically created the still-popular genre of historical fiction and gave its name to Edinburgh's main terminal.

CAN YOU DIG IT?

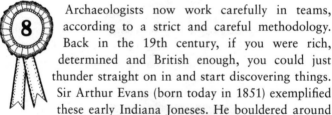

Archaeologists now work carefully in teams, according to a strict and careful methodology. Back in the 19th century, if you were rich, determined and British enough, you could just thunder straight on in and start discovering things. Sir Arthur Evans (born today in 1851) exemplified these early Indiana Joneses. He bouldered around exotic locations and discovered many remarkable treasures such as the palace of Knossos on Crete and the entire Minoan civilisation. He was knighted for his discoveries.

WIMBLEDON SERVES UP

The Championships, Wimbledon, is the oldest tennis tournament in the world and the most prestigious. It has been held at the All England Club in the London suburb of Wimbledon since this day in 1877 and is the only major championship still played on grass. And quite right too. When Major Walter Clopton Wingfield invented the game during a party on his estate in Llanelidan, Wales, in 1873, it was on his garden lawn.

Major Walter Clopton Wingfield

SPACE AGE TV

10 Telstar, the first satellite to supply a live transatlantic television feed, and the first privately sponsored space launch, was sent into orbit today in 1962. It was co-designed by the British General Post Office and internationally co-ordinated from BBC Television Centre in London. It also successfully relayed through space the first telephone calls and fax images.

WHAT A LOO

11 Waterloo Station (opened today in 1848) is one of the world's biggest and busiest stations, with 88 million passengers a year passing through its barriers. That's over 240,000 travellers a day (in case you don't have a calculator to hand). Until 2009, the station even had its own police station, with three cells. It is also the Northern Line underground station for those wishing to visit the extremely popular tourist attraction, the London Eye.

And, of course, its name derives from the scene of a famous British victory, Wellington's defeat of Napoleon in 1815.

NEW TYPE OF NOVEL DETECTED

The Moonstone, by Wilkie Collins, was published today in 1868 and almost single-handedly launched one of the most popular of all fiction genres: the detective novel. Collins' tale includes several elements that would become staples of this type of story, including a robbery in a country house, a skilled investigator, bungling local plods, red herrings, a 'locked room' murder and a twist in the tail.

WHO'S WHOM

Readers of the *St James's Chronicle* in 1780 would this morning have seen this advertisement: 'John Debrett begs leave most respectfully to acquaint the Nobility and Gentry and his readers in general that he is removed from the late Mr William Davis's the corner of Sackville Street to Mr Almon's Bookseller and Stationer, opposite Burlington House, where he hopes he shall be honoured with their commands.' The ad obviously worked: this is the same Debrett whose name has for more than two centuries adorned the reference tome of *the* British nobility. And if you need to check – no, you aren't in it.

HERE'S LOOKING AT YOU ...

14 Marie Tussaud (born Anna Maria Grosholtz) was French, and she honed her waxwork-making skills by making death masks from the decapitated heads of executed citizens during the French Revolution. But it was in Britain that she established her legendary waxwork museum, which took up residence in its famous building on the Marylebone Road in London today (Bastille Day, appropriately enough) in 1884.

GET YOUR BROLLIES OUT

15 Swithun was a 9th-century Bishop of Winchester who was canonised for miraculously restoring some broken eggs. Wow. Legend says that the weather on his feast day (today) will continue for 40 days. Modern science backs up this old tale: around now the jet stream settles into a pattern that usually holds steady until the end of August. If it lies north of Britain, then continental high pressure can move in, otherwise wet Atlantic weather systems take charge.

THE NOT-SO SECRET SERVICE

 For eighty years, no one had even admitted that one of our greatest British institutions existed (despite everyone knowing full well that it did), then today in 1993 the Secret Service decided to blow its own cover. Stella Rimington became MI5's first Director General to pose for the cameras as she launched a brochure outlining the organisation's activities. When MI5 later began advertising job vacancies, it received 12,000 applications on the first day.

THE PERFECT PUNCHLINE

It's thanks to *Punch* that today we refer to a humorous illustration as a 'cartoon'. The famous British magazine first appeared today in 1841 and was hugely influential for most of its life until it faded out in the 1990s. Its gentle, sophisticated wit was enjoyed by readers from Charlotte Brontë to Queen Victoria; it could boast Charles Dickens as an editor and on its drawing staff were E.H. Shepard (who illustrated *Winnie the Pooh*) and John Tenniel (who illustrated *Alice in Wonderland*).

X MARKS THE VOTE

18 Voting could be a boisterous business before this day in 1872. Landowners virtually ruled their employees, and so could direct their vote, either by standing over them at the ballot or sending an agent to do so. They could also bribe independent voters, many of whom took bungs from both sides. Then the Prime Minister, William Gladstone, introduced secret ballot voting and, although some landowners decried it for being 'unmanly', it ushered in a fairer democratic system.

ENGINEERING EXCELLENCE

19 When it comes to building revolutionary machines, there is one Brit who is particularly great: Isambard Kingdom Brunel. He built bridges (including the Clifton Suspension Bridge), dockyards and the Great Western Railway, for which he designed the viaducts, tunnels, stations and even the locomotives. He constructed the first tunnel under a river (the Thames Tunnel), his *Great Britain* was the first steamship driven by a screw propeller while the *Great Western* (launched today in 1837) was the largest and fastest ship in the world and made the transatlantic voyage in record time.

SWAN UPPING

Today sees the completion of the very bizarre tradition of 'swan upping' on the River Thames. Five days ago, men from the Dyers' and Vintners' Companies of the City of London piled into rowing boats and set off from Sunbury on a 70-mile voyage to Abingdon. On the way, they surrounded all the swans they saw, caught them, counted them and then released them.

You might wonder what the point of this is, after all, it's not like the elegant creatures are endangered or even in scarce numbers. Well, British people have been doing it since the 12th century; it's a British tradition and that's all there is to it.

INTRODUCING THE MCCURRY

Chicken Tikka Masala is one of Britain's favourite foods, but it's not a traditional Indian dish: it's claimed a Bangladeshi chef in Glasgow cooked a dish of orthodox chicken tikka only to have the customer ask, 'Where's my gravy?' He promptly improvised a sauce with a can of tomato soup, some cream and a few spices, and *voila!* Instant masala. And today in 2009, MP Mohammad Sarwar tabled a motion in Parliament for Glasgow to be given European Union Protected Designation of Origin status for the dish. Remember that, next time you order one from your local Indian restaurant!

PLIMSOLL'S OUTBURST

22 Bellowing in rage at the Prime Minister is something most of us do in private, but when Samuel Plimsoll did it in Parliament today in 1875, it helped pass a new law that saved thousands of sailors' lives.

Plimsoll wanted to stop overloaded ships putting to sea and was angry because his Merchant Shipping Act was being scuttled by ship-owning MPs. His outburst worked, and the Act was passed. It established, among other safety measures, the mark indicating a ship's loading limit, known now as the Plimsoll line.

REIGN OF THE SPEED KING

23 Today in 1955, Surrey-born speed king Donald Campbell set his first world record when he shot across Ullswater in his jet-boat *Bluebird K7* at 202.15 mph. He would go on to break more water speed records than anyone else, and to become the only person to break the land and water speed records in the same year (1964). Campbell died when *Bluebird* crashed during another record attempt in 1967.

PUKKA CHUKKA

Modern polo wasn't invented in Britain (it originated in India) but we certainly popularised it and turned it into the high-society happening it is famous for being today. Cowdray Park in West Sussex is the spiritual home of British polo and the venue for the Gold Cup, the sport's premier trophy. The Park held its first tournament today in 1910.

COFFEE AND CAT FOOD

British engineer Christopher Cockerell was experimenting with a coffee tin and a cat food tin, placing one inside the other and blasting air into the gap between them with a hair dryer, when he discovered something interesting – a high-pressure cushion of air gave the cans unexpected lift. He used this concept to create the modern hovercraft, which made its famous crossing of the Channel today in 1959. The Duke of Edinburgh insisted on taking the wheel when inspecting the invention, and badly dented the craft.

WHAT A CARRY ON, NURSE

26 It's easy to moan about the queue in A&E when you've just shut your finger in your car door, but looking at things from a global perspective, the National Health Service (NHS) is still something to be proud of. The concept of free medical care for all was spearheaded by Aneurin Bevan, who became Minister of Health today in 1945. It's an idea we're comfortable with now, but at the time it caused a ruckus. Bevan faced opposition from Conservatives, the British Medical Association and members of his own party. After 18 months of bickering, the NHS finally bandaged its first finger in 1948.

THE TORCH COMES TO LONDON - AGAIN

27 When the games of the XXX Olympiad commence on this day in 2012, it will be the third time that London has hosted the Summer Olympics (they were also here in 1908 and 1948). No other city has done so. If you were one of the lucky people to get tickets for any of the events (millions of people applied, millions of people were disappointed) then today you'll be at Olympic Park, East London having, hopefully, an olympic-sized day out.

COMET SENSE

28 If you can hang on until today in 2061, you can watch the return of the comet named after one of Britain's greatest astronomers, Edmond Halley. He was the first man to work out that comets return regularly: the comet seen in 1682 was the same one that had appeared in 1607 and 1531. He predicted it would return in 1758, but died 16 years before he was proved right. The comet named after him is one of the nippiest things in the solar system, clocking 157,838 mph.

LE TUNNEL

29 Admittedly, we can only take half the credit, as the French started digging from their end too, but the Channel Tunnel is still an impressive achievement. Margaret Thatcher and François Mitterrand signed the agreement today in 1987, and seven years later the first passengers were travelling *'sous la Manche'*. Now around 17 million people use the tunnel every year. At 23.5 miles, it has the longest undersea portion of any tunnel in the world and is 31.4 miles long overall.

PAPERBACKS BREAK OUT

30 Readers the world over have been tucking battered paperbacks into their jacket pocket for decades now. But that wasn't possible before today in 1935 when the first Penguin paperback appeared. Costing just 6d, it put a quality read within everyone's reach, and within a year one million Penguin books had been sold.

BULLY FOR YOU

31 On this day in 1712, just five years after the Act of Union between England and Scotland, a Scottish satirist called John Arbuthnot created the archetypal Brit. John Bull was a plain-talking, hard-drinking farmer in a Union Jack waistcoat with a bulldog by his side. Fond of country sports, he was honest, generous, stubborn, had a zest for life and was ready to fight for what he believed in.

For some reason, it's an image that has stood the test of time.

AUGUST

RULE, BRITANNIA!

This popular British national song was originally included in *Alfred*, a masque about Alfred the Great, which was first performed today in 1740, to commemorate the accession of George II. The lyrics themselves originated from a poem written by James Thomson, then set later to the stirring music by Thomas Arne.

It's a proud song, patriotic for sure, with a healthy dose of plucky pomp. But if you're going to bellow it at the top of your lungs in a public arena, while waving the Union Jack, you should at least remember to get the words right. So, the original chorus, as it was written, should go like this:

Rule, Britannia![1] Britannia rule[2] the waves:
Britons never will[3] be slaves.

[1] Note the comma and exclamation mark.
[2] Not 'rules'.
[3] Not 'shall'.

HUDSON FINDS HIS BAY (SORT OF)

2 Henry Hudson was one of the greatest, and most unsung, of all British explorers. Today in 1610, he discovered the huge bay, twice the size of the Baltic Sea, which bears his name. The Hudson River in New York is also named after him, as are Hudson County, the Henry Hudson Bridge, the Hudson Strait and the town of Hudson, New York. His obscurity is possibly because he actually thought Hudson Bay was the Pacific Ocean and his crew got so hacked off that they cast him and his son adrift, never to be seen again.

EXPLORING THE COSMIC PLANE

3 Today in 1904, Briton Francis Younghusband trod new ground when he became one of the first Westerners ever to enter the forbidden city of Lhasa. Unfortunately, he was a bit rough with the locals, but took on some Eastern karma to make amends. He had a mystical experience which suffused him with 'love for the whole world'. He became a sort of proto-hippy who believed in the power of cosmic rays, and claimed that there are extraterrestrials with translucent flesh on the planet Altair.

A GREAT WAY TO GET IN FREE

If you've ever passed out in sheer delirium at a Take That gig, you probably have the British Red Cross to thank for your subsequent recovery. Founded today in 1870, its original goal was to provide aid to the belligerents on both sides of the Franco-Prussian War. Now they have over 31,000 volunteers and 2,600 staff providing help to people in crisis, both in the UK and overseas. And they provide more first aid at concerts than anyone else in the world.

SPITFIRE STARTS UP

The Supermarine Spitfire became legendary during the Battle of Britain and it first flew into service today in 1938. It was a superbly designed fighting machine; highly manoeuvrable with great acceleration and a top speed of 400 mph. More Spitfires have been produced than any other British aircraft (20,351) and it was the only Allied fighter in production throughout the war. It also looks so cool.

WORLD WIDE WEB CLICKS INTO ACTION

The Internet is a global system of linked computer networks, and its origins date back to the 1960s as a US defence tool, as well as a quicker way of connecting university libraries together. The World Wide Web, in comparison (and to much confusion), is made up of the websites that people 'surf' and contains the images, text and videos we all enjoy and share. The World Wide Web was created by British physicist Tim Berners-Lee, who promptly gave the patent of its use to the world for free, after the first ever webpage went online today in 1991.

BROOM-BROOM BROOKLANDS

There have been many dazzling, and superb, circuits built since but Brooklands in Surrey was the world's first permanent racing circuit, and it held its first ever Grand Prix today in 1926. Unfortunately, the race was won by the French team, but nevermind. The legendary banked oval track could house 250,000 spectators and was the preferred venue for many early Land Speed Record attempts.

ARMS AND THE ARMADA

The Spanish Armada of 151 ships aimed to overthrow Elizabeth I. But it met a stalwart defence today in 1588 near the port of Gravelines in Flanders. The English Navy used their more manoeuvrable ships and bold tactics (including using fire ships) to rout the Armada and chase it into the North Sea. Severe storms also savaged the Spanish and, of the 151 ships that made up the fleet, only around 67 made it back to Spain. The victory marked a lasting shift in world naval balance in England's favour.

BRIGHTON BARES ALL

Today in 1979, Brighton became the first major resort in Britain to have a nudist beach. Which is notable, considering how flipping freezing our summers tend to be. Frankly, any Britons who go completely nude on Britain's beaches deserve a medal, although working out where to pin it could be tricky.

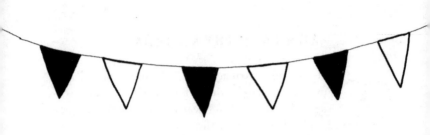

FIRST NIGHT OF THE PROMS

 The 'Last Night of the Proms' might be a little bit too British for many people. But the promenade concerts aren't really about flag-waving. When impresario Robert Newman organised the first concert today in 1895, he actually aimed to attract people from all walks of life, particularly those who might not normally appreciate classical music. His proms had low prices and an informal atmosphere where eating, drinking and smoking were encouraged.

His tradition continues today: the prom season has over 100 concerts in auditoriums and parks across the UK, as well as educational and children's events.

NICE ASCOT

11 Royal Ascot is such a glamorous social event that coverage of people's attire far exceeds racing news. The privileged few invited into the Royal Enclosure must obey a strict dress code: morning dress with top hat for gentlemen, while ladies must wear a dress that doesn't reveal too much flesh. But the more fabulous and over-the-top your hat, the better. Over the years, there have been some utterly ridiculous ones.

The first ever Royal Ascot horse race was held on this day in 1711 and now more than 300,000 people come to make a splash during Royal Ascot week.

MORE THAN JUST A MOUTHWASH

Today in 1865, 11-year-old James Greenness was admitted to hospital with a compound fracture of his leg. The very high risk of infection in those days made that a potential death sentence. But, luckily for James, the doctor treating him was Joseph Lister, who was about to make a monumental medical breakthrough. Lister wondered if clean hands and instruments and a swab of a 5 per cent carbolic acid solution might help prevent infection. Young James was his guinea pig.

The boy made a full recovery and the medical world had antiseptics.

BREARLEY CLEANS UP

In 1913, Sheffield metallurgist Harry Brearley was trying to prevent rifle barrels from corroding, and was experimenting by dissolving them in acid. He noticed that steel with a high chromium content didn't dissolve. After researching varying proportions, today Harry produced an alloy with 12.8 per cent chromium, which he called 'rustless steel'. This was later changed to 'stainless steel' and a whole new metal industry was born.

BEACH BEAUTIES

After the strict morality and decorum of the Victorian era, the Edwardian age brought a little more daring and frivolity, like the first ever beauty contest, which was held today at the Pier Hippodrome in 1908 in Folkestone. Despite containing entrants from all over the world, it was a local 18-year-old girl from East Molesey Nellie Jarman, who swept the judges off their sandy feet. Of course, since the bikini wouldn't be invented for another 38 years, it wasn't *that* daring a contest. But jolly good fun all the same.

THE MODERN KILT TAKES OFF

The kilt is Scottish, of course, rather than British, but its current popularity as a symbol of Scotland is a story with influences from all over the UK.

Highland dress was banned in 1746 after the second Jacobite uprising. It became a romantic symbol of an oppressed people. In the early 19th century, writer Sir Walter Scott was helping revive the tradition and, when King George IV visited Edinburgh today in 1822 wearing a kilt, the draughty garment made a swirling comeback.

SUBTEXT

Before today in 1858, it took at least ten days for a message to cross the Atlantic. But now it took a matter of minutes thanks to the first transatlantic telegraph, which was inaugurated by Queen Victoria and US President James Buchanan. The system failed after a month and it took seven years to convince sceptical investors to fund the repair. And you thought waiting in all day for BT to come round was bad.

LICK IT AND SEE

Whatever you think of the Royal Mail now, in the 1830s it was much, much worse. Letters were paid for by the recipient, who could simply refuse delivery, and you paid more the further the letter went. Bad news if Granny lived in Orkney.

Then Rowland Hill had a brilliant idea: low and uniform rates based on weight and the prepayment of postage, receipted with a stamp and today in 1839 the Postage Act was passed. In May the following year, the Penny Black, the world's first adhesive postage stamp, appeared on letters.

OASIS GO SUPERSONIC

 Oasis were the power behind the Britpop music boom of the 1990s and they played their first ever live gig today in 1991 at the Boardwalk club in Manchester. Noel Gallagher wasn't in the band yet – he was still a roadie for Inspiral Carpets – and he only went to the gig to check out his younger brother's band. He suddenly realised that with the addition of his songs the band could go far. Within a few years, they would become one of the best-selling British bands of all time with over 40 million records sold.

READY, STEADY, COE!

There was a time when Britain left the rest of the world standing on the track. That dominance pretty much started today in 1979 when Sebastian Coe completed an incredible hat-trick. In July, he had bagged the 800-metre and mile world records and today he also became the fastest man ever to run the 1500 metres. With the Steves Ovett and Cram hot on his heels, golden days were ahead for British athletics.

DARWIN CHANGES THE WORLD

As ideas go, Charles Darwin's concept of adaptation by natural selection has to be one of the most important and far-reaching that anyone has ever had. The theory that would later become *On the Origin of Species* was first published today in 1858 and, although it was derided (and considered controversial) by many people, this work is now the cornerstone of modern evolutionary understanding. Since the theory has become embraced widely (though not universally just yet) the world will look back at Darwin's acheivements as the day all life on Earth started to understand where it came from.

NO LADDER IN HER TIGHTS

Today in 1976, Mary Langdon of Sussex became the first ever British firewoman. That might seem like a slow response to changing times, but Britain is actually one of the most progressive countries when it comes to emergency equality. We now have more than 200 full-time women firefighters and another 200 serving as retained firefighters.

CAMPAIGN FOR REAL ALE

Holding a tasty pint of real ale in your hand – as opposed to fizzy European lager or weak America beer – is one of those magical feelings that you simply don't get anywhere else in the world ... and is a truly British tradition. Real ale usually looks like thick muddy water, and often called ridiculous names like Piston Bitter, Bishop's Finger and Old Speckled Hen, but also has a depth of flavour that always warms the cockles. And thanks to Bill Mellor, Graham Lees, Michael Hardman and Jim Makin, who held CAMRA's (Campaign for Real Ale) first AGM today in 1972 at the Rose Inn, Nuneaton the proper ale drinking tradition is set to continue long into the future. Though details of this first meeting are a little hazy...

FRINGE BENEFITS

23 The Edinburgh International Festival aimed to celebrate the best in the performing arts when it first got under way today in 1947, but was quickly gatecrashed by unofficial performers who created the much edgier 'Fringe'. Now the whole thing is called the Edinburgh Festival and is the largest cultural event in the world. The great thing about the Fringe is that anyone can book a venue and take part. Just don't expect instant fame – the average Fringe audience numbers nine people.

A CORKER OF AN IDEA

24 Being an inventive nation is something to celebrate, particularly when what we've come up with is a better way to open wine bottles. And today in 1795, Samuel Henshall was awarded patent number 2061 for his improved corkscrew. This revolutionary design used a button between the shank and the worm to free the cork and make it pull more smoothly.

Cheers, Samuel!

NICE DAY FOR A DIP

The English Channel is the busiest stretch of water in the world, but that hasn't stopped people wanting to swim across it. The 21-mile gap across the Strait of Dover is far enough to be a huge physical challenge, while close enough to be possible. The first person to achieve the feat was Captain Matthew Webb, who hauled himself out on to a French beach on this day in 1875. His crossing took 21 hours and 45 minutes. The current record is 6 hours 57 minutes 50 seconds, set by Bulgarian Petar Stoychev in 2007.

LONGBOWS BECOME LEGENDARY

The military supremacy of the English longbow was established on this day in 1346 at the Battle of Crécy. The French had a huge force of up to 100,000 men against the English and Welsh army of 15,000, but they placed too much strategic importance on their armoured knights and crossbowmen. The longbowmen could fire faster and more accurately and, when the knights became literally bogged down, the French were vanquished.

A QUICK WAR BEFORE BREAKFAST

27 If you're going to have a war, best make it a quick one. And today in 1896 saw Britain win the world's shortest ever conflict – the Anglo-Zanzibar War. This fracas lasted approximately 38 minutes, from 9.02 a.m. when British gunships opened fire on the Sultan of Zanzibar's palace, to 9.40 a.m. when he decided it was probably wise to surrender.

CARNIVAL CHRISTENED

28 Nowadays up to 2 million people throng London's Notting Hill for the largest street carnival in Europe. But today in 1964 less than a hundred enjoyed the inaugural party. It started when a group of Trinidadian immigrants decided to throw an impromptu carnival procession through their neighbourhood, complete with steel band. The spectacle caught the public eye and the seeds of the current Carnival were sown.

CHARGED WITH BRILLIANCE

29 Michael Faraday was a humble blacksmith's son who happened to be a scientific genius. Today in 1831, he discovered electromagnetic induction – how a change in magnetic intensity can produce an electric current. Soon after, he discovered that electricity was generated when a magnet passed through a helix wound with wire. He thus invented the transformer and dynamo, key elements of the electric motor. It was largely thanks to Faraday that electricity could be put to practical use.

SUCCESS IS IN THE BAG

30 Sometimes being British sucks. And, that couldn't be any truer for Hubert Cecil Booth, who today in 1901 patented the first powered vacuum cleaner. Booth got his big break, and recognition, when his machine was used to clean the carpets of Westminster Abbey before Edward VII's coronation. But his device was so large it had to be pulled from house to house *by a horse*. Obviously, that was never going to be a popular household product, so it wasn't until an American upstart, called Hoover, built a smaller machine that the house-tidying business started to clean up.

BOWLER BORN

 When William Coke asked his London hatter James Lock to make him a new hat, he specified a bold design: it had to be close-fitting, lower than a top hat and very strong. Coke's uncle was the Earl of Leicester and he wanted a practical hat to protect the heads of the family's gamekeepers. Two hatmakers, or milliners as they are technically known, were commissioned to fulfil the order: Thomas and William Bowler. And very soon the world – but more importantly Britain – had one of the most recognisable fashion items of all time. The Bowler hat is also one of the most popular images associated with Britain, along with the tea pot, umbrellas and bunting. To this day, Lock & Co still make bowler hats.

SEPTEMBER

IT'S BAD FOR YOU, YOU KNOW

It seems obvious now, but before this day in 1950, people had no concrete evidence that smoking was linked to lung cancer and heart disease. In fact, tobacco companies often highlighted their products' health *benefits*. Then physiologist Richard Doll (with Austin Hill) studied lung cancer patients in 20 London hospitals and discovered that smoking was the only factor they had in common. Doll stopped smoking himself and today published his findings in the *British Medical Journal*.

POUR ON WATER

The Great Fire of London, which started today in 1666, was tragic for the city's inhabitants but it was probably a good thing for Britain in the long run. London had been a filthy, overcrowded warren of a capital; the fire incinerated many slums and all traces of the previous year's plague, and the devastation allowed the capital to be rebuilt in brick and stone, not wood. The new streets were wider and cleaner and many beautiful new public buildings were created, including St Paul's Cathedral.

FLEMING DISCOVERS PENICILLIN

Don't you hate it when you come back from holiday to find the place in a mess? Alexander Fleming certainly did when he returned to his laboratory today in 1928 – there were contaminated bacteria cultures all over his workbench. Luckily, though, while he was away, a fungus had killed patches of bacteria. Fleming was amazed and he soon developed that fungus into penicillin, the most efficacious life-saving drug in the world. It would conquer syphilis, gangrene and tuberculosis among many other infections, saving an estimated 200 million lives to date.

THE MODS ARE HERE

With their sharp suits, Italian scooters, distinctive hairstyles and music tastes, Mods were a major part of British youth culture in the 50s, 60s and 70s. 'Mods' came from 'modernists', reflecting the group's origins among young fans of 'modern' jazz. The term encompassed a whole subculture, but the movement was first brought to a wider audience in Colin MacInnes' cult novel *Absolute Beginners*, which was published today in 1959.

RIDER READY, PEDALS READY, GO

Today in 1839, Scottish blacksmith Kirkpatrick Macmillan fitted cranks to the rear-wheel axle of a dandy horse (a two-wheeled vehicle the rider pushed along with their feet on the ground) and connected them with rods to foot pedals. In doing so, he created one of the world's great inventions – the pedal cycle. He later fitted a steering mechanism to the front wheel and set off for a spin. His first long-distance journey was to Glasgow, 70 miles from his home. It was a success, although it did take two days and cost him a five-shilling fine when he knocked over a startled pedestrian.

TANKS FOR THE MEMORIES

A new era in military history dawned on this day in 1915 when the first ever tank rolled off the production line of the Wellington Foundry in England. Weighing 16.5 tonnes, it was 26 feet long, had a scorching top speed of 2 mph and was nicknamed 'Little Willie' after the press's mocking term for the German Imperial Crown Prince Wilhelm.

GRACE, OUR DARLING

Some Britons are so brave it takes your breath away. Grace Darling was the daughter of a lighthouse keeper from Bamburgh, Northumberland. A savage storm forced the steamship *Forfarshire* aground today in 1838 and broke the vessel up, stranding nine people on a rock offshore amid giant waves. Twenty-two-year-old Grace calmly got into a boat with her father and rowed over a mile through mountainous seas to rescue the sailors and, in the process, become a national heroine.

DR SNOW BRAVES CHOLERA TO SAVE THOUSANDS

8 In 1854 cholera outbreaks killed thousands in Britain's cities. People thought the disease spread by 'bad air' and did little to halt its progress. Dr John Snow thought differently and took to the streets of Soho to investigate. By carefully mapping the cases, he discovered that a water pump in Broad Street was the centre of the outbreak. A cesspit had contaminated the well. Today, he begged authorities to remove the pump's handle; they were sceptical, but did so. The outbreak faded away.

Snow's work was one of the biggest events in the history of public health and helped to found the science of epidemiology.

THE FLYING POSTIE

9 Britain notched up another pioneering achievement today in 1911, when the world's first scheduled airmail post service took off. It may only have linked the London suburb of Hendon with Windsor in Berkshire but, then again, it was only 1911.

THE 'COUGHING MAJOR' CLEANS UP

When Major Charles Ingram won the top prize on *Who Wants To Be A Millionaire?* today in 2001, some ne'er-do-wells had the temerity to suggest that his chum in the audience, Tecwen Whittock, had signalled the correct answers to him by coughing. As if a major in the British Army would possibly ever cheat at anything! Poppycock! No, today we celebrate Major Ingram's brains, bravado and say, 'Jolly well done, old man!'

GOOD NEWS FOR PANDAS

Today in 1961, the World Wildlife Fund opened its doors to our furred and feathered friends. The WWF (renamed the World Wide Fund for Nature in 1986) is now the world's largest independent conservation organisation with over 5 million supporters worldwide. It supports around 1,300 conservation and environmental projects, making a lot of happy pandas.

GETTING THE POINT

12 Cleopatra's Needle may be one of Britain's best-loved monuments, but it's also the most badly named. Erected on the Thames Embankment today in 1878, the 68-foot, 224-ton red granite obelisk was gifted to us by Egypt to commemorate victories at the Battle of the Nile in 1798 and the Battle of Alexandria in 1801. But the obelisk is almost 3,500 years old, meaning it was already ancient by the time Queen Cleopatra VII came to the throne.

BESSEMER FORGES AHEAD

13 Iron is strong but brittle. By the 1850s, several iron bridges had collapsed with disastrous consequences, and engineers longed to be able to use steel. This is more malleable, but it was also then very expensive. Sir Henry Bessemer, after years of experimentation, today in 1856 generously published details of his eponymous steel-making process in *The Times*. It created the cheaper steel that fuelled a worldwide wave of train- and shipbuilding and made Bessemer very rich indeed.

HANDEL TURNS IT ON

Today in 1741, after just 24 days of inspired composing, George Frideric Handel finished his *Messiah*, a monumental musical masterpiece. Written in English, it is one of the world's most popular oratorios and its 'Hallelujah' chorus is a particular Christmas favourite.

BATTLE OF BRITAIN DAY

The Battle of Britain was an air campaign launched by the Luftwaffe against the United Kingdom during the summer and autumn of 1940. Its aim was to destroy the RAF to clear the way for an invasion of Britain.

For three and a half months, German bombers targeted airfields, docks and cities as fighter pilots battled it out in deadly dogfights. But the Luftwaffe had underestimated the RAF's resources and capabilities. Today's major air engagements marked a crucial turning point in the battle.

THE *MAYFLOWER* SETS SAIL

16 In 1620, King James I was making life uncomfortable for people of non-conformist religions. On this day, 102 men, women and children, many of whom were Puritans, sailed from Plymouth aboard the *Mayflower*, seeking a freer life in the New World.

After 65 gruelling days at sea, they landed at what is now called Plymouth Rock in Massachusetts. The 'Pilgrim Fathers' became the first permanent European settlers in America and helped shape the future democracy of the United States.

WATER WAY TO GO, NORMAN

Britain is stuffed with eccentrics, but very few are actually world-beaters. Step forward Norman Buckley, who today in 1956 broke the one-hour world water speed record in his motorboat, *Miss Windermere III*. Norman was remarkable because he was actually a 48-year-old solicitor from Manchester who only designed, built and raced his all-conquering hydrofoil in his spare time.

CORNY, BUT TRUE

The Corn Laws were a 19th-century price-fixing scam – the big players made money at the expense of everyone else. It wasn't fair, but it was just the way things were done. Then Richard Cobden and John Bright formed the Anti-Corn Law League today in Manchester in 1838. They achieved their titular goals eight years later, helping to establish a fully free-trade economy and boosting international trade. It also meant ordinary people paid less for a loaf of bread.

'IT'S NOT FOR GAMES...'

Clive Sinclair founded his revolutionary electronics company today in 1973, and within a few short years he put Britain at the forefront of home computing. His ZX80, brought out in 1980, had a tiny 1 KB of memory (it would take a million of them to match today's average laptop), but cost just £99.95, bringing it within reach of the average household for the first time. Two years later, Sinclair launched the ZX Spectrum; kids persuaded their parents they needed one for school, it became Britain's best-selling computer and a whole generation of brilliant boffins was born.

TOO POSH TO WASH

Every efficiency counted back in the dark days of 1942, and today every household was asked to bathe in no more than five inches of water to conserve fuel. This might have kicked up a dirty old ruckus had not the Royal Family instantly announced that they had painted black lines on all their baths to keep water levels low, no matter how mucky the monarchy got.

TA, MAC!

Next time you're stuck in a 12-mile tailback on the M25, don't despair – take pride! The road you are not moving very fast on is the work of a great British pioneer, John McAdam. Born today in 1756, he revolutionised road construction the world over by using tar to bind the surface's stones together and create a smoother, harder, and more practical, road surface. The word 'tarmac' even comes from 'tar Macadam'.

OPEN HOUSE AT NUMBER 10

Today in 1735, Robert Walpole became the first British Prime Minister to live at 10 Downing Street. Number 10 is larger than it looks – it was originally three houses. King George II offered them to Walpole, who accepted the gift on the condition that it was for his position rather than for him personally. He then had the three houses joined together and the extended residence has been the Prime Minister's ever since.

ROW, ROW, ROW YOUR BOAT

Today in 2000, Steve Redgrave won gold at his fifth consecutive Olympic Games. With him in his coxless four were Matthew Pinsent (winning gold at his third consecutive Games), Tim Foster and James Cracknell. The men were cheered on by 22,000 delirious British fans as they pipped the Italians into second place by just 0.38 seconds. Redgrave was knighted the next year and has a fair claim to be Britain's greatest Olympian.

CROSS OF HONOUR

The George Cross is the mark of a true British hero. Instituted today in 1940, it is the highest civilian decoration of the United Kingdom, the equivalent of the military's Victoria Cross, and is only awarded 'for acts of the greatest heroism or of the most conspicuous courage in circumstances of extreme danger'. So far, there have been 155 ultimate heroes, 84 of whom received their award posthumously.

GREEN FOR GO

25 No one flies the flag faster than Wing Commander Andy Green, who today in 1997 clocked an incredible 714.144 mph (1,149.30 km/h) in his jet-powered car, ThrustSSC. He later raised this record to 763.035 mph, becoming the first man to break the sound barrier on land.

HAIR RAISING

26 Today in 1968, Britain pioneered a new era of cultural freedom with the abolition of theatre censorship. The new Theatres Act ended the Lord Chamberlain's powers of censorship, which dated back to 1737. The very next day, the hippy musical *Hair*, which featured nudity and drug-taking, opened in London. The countercultural revolution of the late 1960s had broken down another barrier, never to be put up again.

DO THE LOCOMOTION

If it's ever taken you three hours to travel 20-odd miles by train, don't despair – you're part of a great British tradition! Today in 1825, the world's first passenger railway service rolled into history when George Stephenson's steam engine *Locomotion* pulled passengers the 26 miles from Shildon to Stockton via Darlington in just under three hours. This event sparked a railway boom and within 50 years there were 160,000 miles of railways around the world.

RADIO GA-GA

It may seem strange today, but there's a whole generation of Brits for whom the two-week festive *Radio Times* was the most exciting publication of the year. The *Radio Times* first appeared today in 1923, and was launched by the BBC because no newspapers would carry radio listings – they feared that increased listenership would decrease their sales. At one time, it was the biggest-selling magazine in Europe.

NATIONAL ROAST DINNER DAY

29 Many of us set aside one day a week, never mind once a year, to enjoy a roast dinner with all the trimmings, or a Sunday Roast as it is traditionally known in my house. It is, after all, a very British thing to do. A joint of tender meat (usually roast beef), accompanied by roast potatoes, stuffing, vegetables, Yorkshire puddings and home-made gravy, makes the home smell of, well, home. Having a national day of roast dinner eating can only be a good thing, even if it's a good whack of your daily calorie intake (around 850). Roast dinners are enjoyed around the world, though notably less so in France – hence the French insult for British people is *'les rosbifs'* – the roast beefs. To Brits, it's not an insult – in fact, it's a compliment!

ROCK ON

When 24-year-old DJ Tony Blackburn dropped a needle on to The Move's 'Flowers In The Rain' today in 1967, he started a British rock and roll revolution. He was the first DJ to broadcast on the BBC's flagship radio station. Radio 1 brought new music into millions of British bedrooms and became a broadcasting phenomenon as well as a symbol of the British people's consistent love affair with the radio. Over its 40 year history, some of the station's shows have attracted over 20 million listeners (almost half the country in the 1970s), making it the most listened-to station in the world. Despite being aimed at the 15–29 age group, the average age of a Radio 1 listener is 33.

OCTOBER

THIS ONE STARTS OFF A LITTLE QUIET ...

Is there another DJ who gave more cool and respected bands their big British break than John Peel? He first broadcast his Radio 1 show today in 1967 and would continue as a presenter on the station for another 37 years. Famous for his extremely eclectic taste, he would think nothing of playing bands as diverse as The Clash, Captain Beefheart and Elmore James in the same half-hour.

All that is written on his headstone besides his name is the line 'Teenage dreams, so hard to beat' from his favourite song 'Teenage Kicks' by The Undertones. One in a million, and recently voted one of the Britain's greatest public icons.

DEWAR GETS BURNED

Your picnic tea stays piping hot thanks to a brilliant bit of thinking by Scottish physicist Sir James Dewar. Back in 1892, he needed something to keep the liquid gases he was working with at a low temperature. So he created a flask with two reflective vessels, one inside the other, separated by a vacuum to stop heat escaping. Unfortunately, Dewar wasn't clever enough to patent his invention, and today in 1907, two German glass blowers registered the trademark 'Thermos', and made a cool fortune in flasks.

INTERCITY 125 ROLLS OUT

It's difficult to imagine when you've been stuck outside York for two hours, but the InterCity 125 train is actually a great British success. The first one left Paddington for Bristol Temple Meads today in 1976 and, amazingly, arrived three minutes early. The world's fastest diesel train still covers 1,000 miles a day, 7 days a week. Its unique shape is thanks to designer Kenneth Grange, who also created the Kenwood Chef and the parking meter.

ATLANTIC CROSSING

It might seem strange now with the dominance of Boeing, but Britain was a pioneer in the jet airliner industry – the first ever transatlantic jet passenger service was launched today in 1958 by BOAC. Passengers could hop between New York and London on the new de Havilland Comet in the record time of 6 hours and 12 minutes.

WAKLEY HEALS THE WORLD

For nearly two centuries, *The Lancet* has been at the cutting edge of medical knowledge. It was first published today in 1823 by Thomas Wakley, an English surgeon and firebrand reformer. Wakley hated 'quackery' and, as well as establishing the world's first peer-reviewed medical journal, he became a radical MP who campaigned fearlessly against incompetence, privilege and nepotism.

WHOHASN'TDUNITBYNOW?

6 *The Mousetrap* has now reached the point where the very fact that it is a British institution will ensure its continued survival, regardless of any inherent quality. Agatha Christie's murder mystery with a shocking twist ending was first performed today in 1952. It has now clocked up more than 24,000 performances and is still running at the St Martin's Theatre, giving it the longest initial run of any play in history.

Christie, not anticipating its success, gave the rights of the play to her grandson as a birthday present.

IT PAYS TO COPY

7 Before this day in 1806, if you wanted to copy a document, you had to write it out again by hand. Then English inventor Ralph Wedgwood patented carbon paper, one of the most useful office products until the computer. He was financed with a £200 loan from his cousin Josiah Wedgwood (of pottery fame), and in just seven years he had turned this sum into £10,000 in profits.

WHAT TOWER?

When the Post Office Tower opened today in 1965, it was the tallest building in Britain. But because its main purpose was to carry telecommunications traffic, some of which might be sensitive, the tower was officially a secret, and did not appear on Ordnance Survey maps until the 1990s. This despite being 581 feet tall and built in Central London... only in Britain.

FOUR-LEGGED FUN

At its peak in the early 1980s, the sheepdog trial TV show *One Man and His Dog* drew more than 8 million loyal viewers. Which is really rather comforting, somehow. The spectacle has a long and noble history: the UK's first sheepdog trials were held in Bala, Wales, on this day in 1873. More than 300 spectators watched 10 dogs battle it out, with the title of champion being awarded to Tweed, a black and tan collie who apparently had a 'foxy' face.

IT ALL ADDS UP

10 British boffins got us into the history books again today in 1961, when the world's first all-electronic desktop calculator made its debut at the Hamburg Business Equipment Fair. The British Bell Punch/Sumlock Comptometer ANITA (A New Inspiration to Arithmetic/Accounting) may not have had a snappy name, but sales were rapid and ANITA heralded a new era of portable calculating devices that meant no one ever had to work out a mind-bendingly difficult sum in their head again.

GOOD NON-SHOW

11 Today in 1987, an American research team had the temerity to come over here and try to prove the existence of the Loch Ness Monster. They used 24 boats and the latest sonar technology to make the biggest sweep of any freshwater lake in the world. Nessie, of course, did exactly what ought to be done in the face of such an overseas intrusion: kept a low profile. The canny beastie made just enough of a blip on the sonar to keep the tourist dollars coming but refrained from causing a scene.

I COMPUTE, THEREFORE I AM

Alan Turing was a British mathematician and computer science pioneer. He spent World War Two cracking German cipher codes and then moved on to computing, developing the idea of the algorithm and computation and laying the foundations for the invention of the modern computer. Today in 1950, he published a famous paper on artificial intelligence in which he proposed the Turing test: if a machine can answer questions so well that a questioner cannot tell it is not human, then it can be said to have intelligence. No machine has passed the Turing test. Yet.

However, scientists are creating computers and machines all the time that are closing in on that moment. The smartest machine on Earth, currently, is called Watson. It is an IBM computing system with a 'brain' the size of 2,400 personal home computers and a database of around ten million documents.

THE WORLD'S TIMEKEEPERS

A prime meridian is a line of longitude that divides the world into east and west. It helps if you have just one of these, but before this day in 1884 many countries used their own.

Largely because Britain had the most ships and the best charts at the time, the meridian running through the Royal Observatory in Greenwich was established as the line of 0° longitude. The French, unsurprisingly, continued to use their own meridian until 1914.

BATTLE OF HASTINGS

14 Today in 1066, the English army was routed at the Battle of Hastings and King Harold II killed. A bit of a downer if you were English at the time, but from a long-term perspective, it goes down as one of the most formative moments in British history. The Normans changed the language, raised new buildings and reformed the church, bringing a European rather than a Scandinavian influence to bear on English society.

THE HOLLOW MOUNTAIN

15 Opened today in 1965, the Cruachan Dam is a power station with a difference. To start with, it's buried a kilometre underground. Four enormous turbines sit in a turbine hall hewn out of solid rock that's cavernous enough to house the Tower of London. Water rushes down tunnels from a dam high in the hills above to power them.

But the real beauty is that water is also pumped up from the loch below in quiet times, ready to be used when 5 million kettles get flicked on. Cruachan was the world's first reversible pump storage hydro system, and its spectacular tunnels featured in the Bond film *The World Is Not Enough*.

BRONTË BRILLIANCE

The Brontë sisters created some of the most brilliant and best-loved tales in all literature. They suffered universal rejection before Charlotte's *Jane Eyre* was published today in 1847, with Emily's *Wuthering Heights* and Anne's *Agnes Grey* following soon after. Released under male pseudonyms, the books became instant bestsellers. Sadly, all three sisters died early, none of them reaching the age of forty.

ATOMIC ADVANCES

If a new generation of nuclear power helps us create a greener future, Britain will certainly have done its bit. Calder Hall at Sellafield (formerly called Windscale), which opened today in 1956, was the world's first commercial nuclear power station. It produced electricity for 47 years until decommissioned in 2003. There are currently 16 nuclear power stations in the UK with about 440 nuclear reactors in the world – with the overwhelming majority being in the USA. It's no wonder their banners are star spangled.

GURN AND BEAR IT

18 Britain is a bastion of silly traditions. And today's Egremont Crab Fair in Cumbria was established way back in 1267, making it one of the oldest days of fun in the world. Among its many silly harvest festivities is the World Gurning Championships. Simply stick your head through a horse collar, pull the ugliest face you can and you too could go down in history.

MAKE THEE MIGHTIER YET

19 Edward Elgar's 'Pomp and Circumstance March' is the tune that's guaranteed to bring proud Brits to their feet, and it was first played by the Liverpool Orchestral Society today in 1901. It was later given words and turned into the song 'Land of Hope and Glory' which is a regular feature of the Last Night of the Proms. The first time it featured at a Promenade concert, the audience apparently '... rose and yelled ... the one and only time in the history of the Promenade concerts that an orchestral item was accorded a double encore'.

LORD OF ALL PUBLISHING

Writers often create new worlds, but few do it on the scale of English writer J.R.R. Tolkien. The final volume of his *The Lord Of The Rings* was published today in 1955, and the world went daft for dwarves and hobbits. The book went on to become the second-best selling novel ever written, shifting over 150 million copies. (In case you're interested, the best selling is by another Brit – *A Tale Of Two Cities* by Charles Dickens – over 200 million copies.)

A SOLID PIECE OF THINKING

The modern world would look very different if it weren't for concrete. Admittedly, there would be a few less architectural carbuncles, but there would also be more unstable buildings, wobbly bridges and uneven roads. One of the vital ingredients in concrete is Portland cement, which a Leeds bricklayer called Joseph Aspdin patented today in 1824. He ground and burned clay and limestone to create a material that hardens when mixed with water, naming it after the stone quarried from Portland, Dorset.

ROUTEMASTER ROLLS OUT

22 The red Routemaster bus is one of the most recognisable symbols of Britain. And the double-deckers with the open platform became an icon for a good reason: they were extremely well made. The Routemaster made its first appearance at the Earl's Court Motor Show today in 1954, and many were still winding their picturesque way through the capital's streets almost half a century later. It wasn't until December 2005 that the last full service finished, with the very last bus being a number 159 from Marble Arch to Streatham.

IVE A GREAT IDEA

23 Apple is, of course, an American computer company, but it owes a large part of its recent success to a Brit. Jonathan Ive is the brilliant designer who was tasked with engineering a hard drive that could store an entire record collection yet be small enough to carry everywhere and also very cool to look at. He rose to the challenge and created the revolutionary iPod, which first appeared today in 2001.

PLAY THE GAME

Grand Theft Auto, which first appeared today in 1997, is one of the most popular and successful video game series of all time. Its famously cool action unfolds in the underworld of several fictional American cities, but the game was actually (and interestingly) developed in Britain, by DMA Design, which later became the legendary Rockstar North.

FOOTBALL KICKS OFF

Today in 1863, 13 football clubs met in London to standardise the laws of the game that would go on to rule the world – association football. The game was very different then – you could legally hack a player to the ground with a sharp kick to the shins if you wanted to, although rolling around like a big girl's blouse afterwards was very much frowned upon.

NO ONE KNOWS WHO THEY WERE...

26 Stonehenge is one of the world's great monuments – and mysteries. The giant sarsen stones of the outer circle weigh up to 50 tons and were brought from 20 miles away, while the 80 bluestones of the inner circle made a 240-mile trip from the Preseli Mountains in Wales.

Today in 1918, Cecil Chubb, the site's owner, passed the 5,000-year-old monument into the nation's care. A good job too – Victorian tourists armed with hammers used to chip off souvenir chunks of the irreplaceable megaliths.

THE GENIUS'S GENIUS

James Clerk Maxwell was a Scottish scientist so brilliant that he was Einstein's hero. He published his first scientific paper at the age of 14 and went on to formulate the Electromagnetic Field Theory, which he first presented today in 1864. These ideas laid the foundation for satellite communications, radio, mobile phones and radar. In his spare time, Maxwell created the first true colour photograph in 1861.

TWINKLE TWINKLE LITTLE SATELLITE

Arthur C. Clarke was a writer of epic science-fiction tales, including *2001: A Space Odyssey*. He also created spectacular science fact when today in 1945 he predicted the existence of the geostationary orbit. This is the belt 22,000 miles above the equator where a satellite will orbit at the same rate as the earth rotates, essentially 'fixing' it above one spot on the ground and allowing more efficient global communication.

SENSE AND SELF-PUBLISHING

29 Jane Austen isn't just one of the most widely read writers in English literature, she also practically created the genre of wry romantic fiction. Her classic books are almost constantly being filmed or adapted into modern settings, and they epitomise the quality British costume drama. *Sense and Sensibility* was her first novel to be published, appearing today in 1811. Like many writers of the time, she had to pay the printer for the privilege.

THE RISE OF THE HEMLINE

30 Some people might think Brits are a stuffy, uptight bunch. And maybe we are. But that makes it all the more amazing when we do decide to shake our booty. Today in 1965 was one such moment, when British model Jean Shrimpton wore a very, very short dress to the Melbourne Cup Carnival and caused a sensation. Soon Mary Quant had perfected the miniskirt and 'Swinging London' was leading the world in fashion and pop culture.

ALLANTIDE

Modern Hallowe'en activities have largely come to us from America, so it's nice that some ancient British traditions have seen a resurgence in recent years. One such is Allantide, which has been celebrated in Cornwall on this day for centuries. Children enjoy scoffing large, highly polished 'Allan apples' and young girls throw walnuts in the fire to determine the fidelity of their future husband. Don't ask how they work it out, I'm not sure. It sounds weird and is slightly eccentric, but it's good British fun and is surely a better tradition for community peace than 'egging' your neighbour's house.

NOVEMBER

PUFFIN POST

Britain beats the world when it comes to eccentrics, a fine example being Martin Harman, who bought the island of Lundy in the Bristol Channel in 1924 and promptly proclaimed himself king. Despite being monarch of just a few dozen people and several thousand seabirds, he had to do things properly, so today in 1929 he issued Lundy's very own set of postage stamps. Their value was in 'Puffins'.

MOTORING INTO THE FUTURE

When Britain got its first full-length motorway with the opening of the M1 today in 1959, it promised a brave new age of driving pleasure. There was no speed limit, no central barrier and, with only 13,000 vehicles a day using the road (rather than today's 88,000), it was probably a jolly pleasant way to get from Watford to Rugby.

THE SEA OF BLACK GOLD

3 A new era in energy dawned today in 1975, when British Petroleum delivered its first oil from the North Sea. This was from the giant Forties field, the largest in the area with an estimated reserve of 5,000 million barrels of crude oil. Its production peaked at an impressive 500,000 barrels a day, and delivered a welcome boost to the economy, but it could never slake our entire national thirst for 1.6 million barrels a day.

YOU WON'T FEEL A THING

4 Dr James Young Simpson's idea of relaxing after dinner was to inhale various chemicals to determine their medical properties. This evening in 1847, he was enjoying just such a recreation with a couple of colleagues when the men found themselves feeling rather jolly. The next thing they knew, the sun was streaming in the window and they were groggily coming back to life.

Simpson had just discovered the anaesthetic effect of chloroform. The medical establishment was sceptical, but he perfected the anaesthetic and, when Queen Victoria used it during labour in 1853, a new era of pain-free surgery began.

THE FALL GUY

Guy Fawkes Night is one of the defining days in the British calendar, when we light bonfires and let off fireworks to celebrate the defeat of the Gunpowder Plot of 1605. Fawkes' attempt to blow up King James I was betrayed and he was caught red-handed with barrels of gunpowder in a cellar under the House of Lords. Sentenced to death, he escaped the agony of being hung, drawn and quartered by jumping from the scaffold and breaking his own neck.

A BRAW BRIDGE

Richard Hannay famously dangled from it in Hitchcock's *The 39 Steps* and today in 1889 construction finished on the Forth Bridge, one of Scotland's most recognisable landmarks. The bridge is a staggering feat of engineering; at the time it had the longest single cantilever bridge span in the world of 1,710 feet. It needed 4,600 men to build it, nearly 100 of whom lost their lives in the process.

TIMES PAST

7 The *London Gazette* is one of the British Government's official journals of record, in which several statutory notices must be published. As such, it's not exactly a riveting read. But it has been published since today in 1665, making it the world's oldest surviving journal and worthy of our respect.

SHUSHING STUDENTS SINCE 1602

8 The Bodleian Library in Oxford is one of the oldest and largest libraries in Europe and was founded today in 1602 when Sir Thomas Bodley donated his books to furnish the nearly defunct university library.

The 'Bod' was the first legal deposit library and its many treasures include the Magna Carta, a Gutenberg Bible and Shakespeare's First Folio. It has 11 million items on 117 miles of shelving.

A NEW TYPE OF THINKING

George Bruce is one of those unsung British inventors who is better known abroad than here. After emigrating to America from Scotland, he revolutionised the printing industry. He obtained the very first design patent to be granted in the US, for his printing fonts (today in 1842), standardised type sizes and created many beautiful typefaces still popular today.

LOVERS OF FREEDOM

Today in 1960 was a turning point in British social history. *Lady Chatterley's Lover* by D.H. Lawrence finally went on sale after winning an obscenity trial that showed just how out of touch the stuffy 'Establishment' was with popular opinion. The prosecution famously asked if the novel were something 'you would even wish your wife or servants to read'. The jury could barely believe the pomposity and promptly gave freedom of speech a much-needed boost. The book sold 3 million copies within three months.

REMEMBRANCE DAY

11 A sombre chapter of British history came to an end at the 11th hour of this 11th day of the 11th month in 1918 as Germany signed the Armistice that ended World War One. Poppies are worn because they flourished in the broken ground of Flanders' fields, and because they symbolise the blood spilled in the conflict.

THE START OF RECORDED HISTORY

12 From The Beatles to Pink Floyd, Radiohead to Lady Gaga – the list of bands who have recorded at Abbey Road is a who's who of world music. EMI bought number 3 Abbey Road, St John's Wood, in 1929 and spent two years transforming it into the world's first custom-built recording studio. Today in 1931, Sir Edward Elgar conducted his famous recording of 'Land of Hope and Glory', played by the London Symphony Orchestra in studio one, and Abbey Road was on its way to becoming the most famous recording studio in the world.

WORLD'S OLDEST BANGERS

The first London–Brighton car run was in 1896 when 54 cars (then new) went for a spin (named The Emancipation Run) to celebrate the raising of the speed limit and the scrapping of the escort with a red flag. But it was today's re-enactment in 1927 that put the eccentric event on the British calendar. Organisers insisted cars must be pre-1905, thereby establishing the London to Brighton Veteran Car Run, now the longest-running motoring event in the world.

AND THIS WEEK'S NUMBER ONE IS...

Before this day in 1952, the nation's top tunes were decided by sales of sheet music. Then Percy Dickens from the *New Musical Express* had the bright idea of asking shops for details of their weekly record sales. He published the first pop chart – of 12 songs – which was topped by Al Martino with 'Here in My Heart'.

THE SHROPSHIRE OLYMPIAN

15 Today in 1850, Dr William Penny Brookes founded The Wenlock Olympian Society at Much Wenlock in Shropshire. This sporting festival (which continues to this day) gave gentlemen the chance to compete in games in the ancient Olympian tradition. Baron Pierre de Coubertin was so impressed when he visited the games in 1890 that he founded the International Olympic Committee and established the modern Olympic movement.

TREASURE BEYOND MEASURE

16 One of the world's most astonishing archaeological discoveries was made today in 1992 when Eric Lawes, a retired gardener and amateur metal detectorist, discovered the 'Hoxne Hoard'. Mr Lawes was looking for a farmer's lost hammer in a field in Sussex when he chanced upon 14,865 Roman coins and jewellery from the 4th century, totalling 7.7 lb of gold and 52.4 lb of silver. It is the largest such collection found anywhere within the Roman Empire. The British Museum paid Mr Lawes and the farmer £1.75 million for their historic discovery.

WE GOT THE WORLD TALKING

As any music fan could tell you, English is the world's favourite international language, seemingly travelled far and wide. This became official today in 1947 when the United Nations made English one of its two working languages (the other being French) and the one most often used. And, with 450 million English speakers worldwide, we Brits have a head start in chatting people up on holiday. However, there are some words that don't travel so well – they are just *too* English. For example, there is one lovely word that you'll, regrettably, rarely hear outside of the country's borders:

BLIMEY

A TRADITIONAL CONTROVERSY ...

Hunting is a very divisive issue: many country people support it; foxes don't. So you can either look on today's vote to ban the sport outright (MPs voted 321 to 204) in 2004 as the needless destruction of a noble and ancient British tradition by an interfering nanny state or the long-overdue abolition of a cruel, and pointless, practice. Either way, it's a notable day in Britain's history. Particularly if you're a fox.

IDEAL LIVING

Our modern obsession with home-makeover shows on television like *Grand Designs* and *DIY SOS* can be traced back to this day in 1908 when the inaugural Ideal Home Exhibition opened at Olympia's grand hall in Kensington. The event was initially cooked up as a marketing stunt for the *Daily Mail*, which sponsored it for 100 years. It is now the biggest home show in the world.

SHERLOCK HOLMES IS DEDUCED

Sherlock Holmes is the most famous detective in literary and cinematic history, and he first appeared in 'A Study In Scarlet', a story featured in *Beeton's Christmas Annual* published today in 1887.

Holmes' powers of close observation and logical deduction were based on author Sir Arthur Conan Doyle's old university professor, Dr Joseph Bell. In his classes, Bell cited the importance of close observation in making a diagnosis. He would often pick a stranger and, by observing him, deduce his occupation and recent activities.

HEAR HEAR, SEE SEE

Today in 1989, the first TV cameras were allowed into the House of Commons and the world could finally see how we British do things in the crucible of democracy. Many MPs objected, fearing it could dumb down their debates. Because all that shouting, insulting, booing and flapping bits of paper at each other is so sophisticated, is it?

SHAKEN, NOT SHTIRRED

Today in 1961 was one of the biggest days in British movie history – 31-year-old Scot Sean Connery was announced as the actor who would play James Bond. Author Ian Fleming initially didn't think much of Connery, calling him 'an overgrown stunt-man'. But he warmed to his performance and gave Bond Scottish ancestry in subsequent novels. Connery, of course, went on to become one of the biggest movie stars of all time and is universally agreed upon as being the world's favourite Bond.

DOCTOR WHO

The nation's young children first hid behind the sofa on this Saturday teatime in 1963 as *Doctor Who* made its debut. The show's Daleks, Autons and Cybermen continued to terrify (and delight) tots for 26 years until the show was cancelled. The Doctor regenerated in 2005, pocketed his sonic screwdriver and climbed back into the TARDIS for more classic time-travelling adventures.

Guinness World Records credits *Doctor Who* as being the longest-running sci-fi TV show of all time.

ALL THE TIME YOU WANT, GENTLEMEN

Throughout most of its history, the Great British pub could open at all hours. As coaching inns, they needed to be available for travellers. It was only with World War One's Defence of the Realm Act that licensing hours were restricted to encourage productivity during the working day. Finally, today in 2005, that outdated nonsense was done away with when 24-hour licensing was introduced. Once again, British people could quaff their favourite tipple whenever they wanted.

MUSICAL MILLIONS

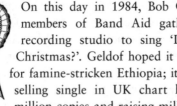

On this day in 1984, Bob Geldof and 43 other members of Band Aid gathered in a London recording studio to sing 'Do They Know It's Christmas?'. Geldof hoped it might raise £70,000 for famine-stricken Ethiopia; it became the biggest-selling single in UK chart history, shifting 3.5 million copies and raising millions of pounds. The effect of Band Aid still resonates now, with Geldof still actively involved in getting the world to listen. In 2005, the massive Live 8 concert in Hyde Park aimed to highlight the continuing struggle in Africa twenty years after the original Live Aid concert.

THE CANAL IN THE SKY

Thomas Telford was one of the greatest of British engineers, designing roads and pioneering bridges such as that over the Menai Strait. He cut his engineering teeth on the famous Pontcysyllte Aqueduct (try saying that five times fast), which opened today in 1805. This beautiful structure carries 1,007 feet of the Llangollen Canal 126 feet above the River Dee valley in North Wales. It is the longest and highest aqueduct in Britain, and a World Heritage Site.

STRIKE A LIGHT

27 Before today in 1826, making fire was fiddly and time-consuming. Then English chemist John Walker mixed up antimony sulfide, potassium chlorate and starch with gum and found it could be struck against any rough surface. He had invented the first friction match, which he called 'Congreves'. Walker refused to patent his revolutionary creation, though no one is sure why – and many sources appear to contradict the other. Some (namely Isaac Asimov) believed Walker thought matches would be so beneficial to mankind that they should remain free to use. However, others believe that it was because Walker deemed them to trivial. His process of making friction matches was later patented by a rival.

STAR STUDENT

28 The detection of pulsars (rapidly spinning and very dense stars) helped confirm part of Einstein's theory of general relativity and has been hailed as the greatest astronomical discovery of the 20th century. The first of these cosmic curios was spotted today in 1967 by Jocelyn Bell Burnell, a postgraduate student from Northern Ireland, using a four-acre radio telescope which she built and operated herself.

NELSON REACHES THE TOP

Vice-Admiral Horatio Nelson was one of Britain's greatest heroes. He worked his way up the ranks to become a captain aged just 20. He personally led boarding parties on enemy ships and won three of the greatest victories in British naval history at the Nile, Copenhagen and Trafalgar. Today in 1843, the stonework of the famous column honouring him in Trafalgar Square was finished. Contrary to myth, neither it nor the real Nelson wore an eye patch.

YOU'RE A SAUCY ONE

If anything goes perfectly with a great British breakfast, it's HP Sauce. This tangy taste-enhancer was perfected today in 1895 by Frederick Garton, a Nottingham grocer. Garton chose 'HP' because he sold a batch to a restaurant in the Houses of Parliament. The original HP factory in Birmingham was later split by the A38(M) so they installed a pipeline that carried vinegar over the motorway.

DECEMBER

CLUELESS?

1 What could be more jolly than sneaking around the ballroom of a country house with your chums and some murder weapons, trying to work out who killed your host? Nothing, according to the millions of fans of Cluedo. The game was patented today in 1944 by Anthony E. Pratt, a solicitor's clerk, who wanted to give people something fun to do during air-raid drills. It was originally called simply 'Murder!'.

ROUGH JUSTICE

Although Britain had long abolished capital punishment for murder, until today in 1997 it was still actually possible by law to be hanged for treason and piracy. However, 2 December finally saw our statute books catch up with the mood of the nation and the punishment was changed to life imprisonment. And besides there are not nearly half as many pirates around, or acts of treason for that matter, as there were when the laws first came into use – around the 1350s.

POTATO PIONEER

Europeans didn't have anything to go with their fish before today in 1586 – that's when Sir Thomas Harriot brought potatoes back to England from America. Harriot was a brilliant astronomer and mathematician who helped Sir Walter Raleigh navigate his way to and from the New World – and spot the potential of the mighty spud. He was also the first person to make a drawing of the moon through a telescope, which he did in July 1609, over four months before Galileo.

AMERICA HAS US TO THANK

 Thanksgiving is one of the USA's biggest national celebrations, but it only exists thanks to 38 colonists from England. Today in 1619, they got out of their boat after landing in the now-called state of Virginia and promptly gave thanks to God for their arrival, an act that many believe started the Thanksgiving tradition.

GOING, GOING, STILL GOING...

James Christie, founder of the famous auction house, brought the hammer down on his first sale today in 1766. He later capitalised on London's new status as the major centre of the international art trade following the French Revolution, building a reputation as the premier auctioneer of fine arts. Christie's has been based at King Street in St James's since 1823.

AARDVARK-ZYMURGY

Today in 1768, the first edition of the *Encyclopædia Britannica* was published, setting the benchmark for scholarly knowledge collection and giving schoolchildren a brilliant place to crib their essays from. The *Britannica* is still going – it is the oldest English-language encyclopedia still in print – but kids nowadays tend to pilfer Wikipedia.

FEELING PRETTY PUMPED

Before this day in 1888, tyres were made from solid rubber, which meant road journeys were pretty bumpy. Then Scottish inventor John Boyd Dunlop patented the first practical inflatable tyre. He initially tested it on his son's tricycle and, when the lad went whizzing happily off, Boyd progressed to bikes and carriages. Within a year, his tyres were sweeping the board at cycle race meetings and travellers were enjoying a smoother ride all round.

DECEMBER

THE RAC GETS INTO GEAR

Inaugurated today in 1897, the Royal Automobile Club has done much to shape the motoring history of Britain. In 1905, the Club organised the first Tourist Trophy (TT) motorcycle race, making that the world's oldest regularly run motor race. It also organised the first British Grand Prix in 1926. The Club also introduced driving certificates in 1905, 30 years before the government decided it was a good idea. It also has one of the largest and most splendid clubhouses in London, on Pall Mall.

AY OOP, CHOOK!

Whether you're a fan or not, you have to admit that *Coronation Street* is a British institution. It first aired today in 1960, making it the world's longest-running TV soap opera currently in production. Few people thought it would run any sort of distance: it got mostly negative reviews and even its makers commissioned only 13 episodes. But viewers loved the believable characters and dramatic storylines. It was also groundbreaking – for many it was the first time they had heard Northern dialect, such as 'nowt' and 'by heck!' at all, let alone on television.

NOBEL PRIZES AWARDED - TO US

Britain is the brainiest nation around – it's official. Today, the prestigious Nobel prizes are awarded and, as of July 2009, an incredible 106 UK brainboxes had received one. This is second only to the USA's 305 brilliant boffins. But, when you consider that the Yanks have 307 million people and we only have 61 million, we clearly have a higher ratio of geniuses in our population.

ADAM'S SENSE OF STYLE

Robert Adam had a lot to live up to, being the son of superstar architect William Adam, but with his brother John he surpassed his father's achievements, becoming a pioneer of the classical revival. The Adam brothers united architecture with interiors, designing walls, ceilings, fireplaces, furniture, fixtures, fittings and carpets. Worldwide he is probably most recognised for Culzean Castle in Ayrshire, which was the setting for the cult classic *The Wicker Man*, released today in 1973.

NORTH ATLANTIC OSCILLATION

12 It was in Britain that Guglielmo Marconi made his name as a pioneer of radio. He sent his first wireless transmission across the Atlantic Ocean today in 1901 at 12.30pm, from Poldhu in Cornwall to Newfoundland, Canada – 2,200 miles away. Often regarded as one of *the* key moments in science, this radio transmission contained just three clicks – or the Morse code signal for 'S'.

SAILING INTO HISTORY

13 Sir Francis Drake was every inch the national hero, repelling the Spanish Armada and becoming the first Briton to circumnavigate the globe. He set out on this historic voyage today in 1577, returning three years later with his *Golden Hind* stuffed full of booty. Queen Elizabeth's half-share of this was more than the crown's other income for that entire year and she promptly knighted him. The Spanish, however, considered him a pirate. And they had a point: it was their treasure he had pinched.

LE PONT BRITANNIQUE

The Millau Viaduct (opened today in 2004) is the tallest bridge in the world, at 1,125 feet. It carries the A75-A71 autoroute over the River Tarn near Millau on its way from Paris to Montpellier. So why should we be proud of it? Well, this stunningly beautiful and technically amazing French masterpiece was designed by British architect Sir Norman Foster. Ooh la la.

WILLIAM HOOKER MOVES TO KEW

William Hooker was a revolutionary botanist who developed the royal pleasure grounds at Kew into the world's foremost botanic gardens. Starting in 1841, he expanded the gardens from 30 to 70 acres and the arboretum to 300 acres, had many new glass-houses erected and established a museum of economic botany.

Kew has the world's largest collection of living plants (over 30,000); research here has helped the commercial cultivation of banana, coffee and tea, and has led to the production of many useful drugs, including quinine.

LUKE HOWARD NAMES THE CLOUDS

We have enough of them, so it makes sense that a Brit should name them – today in 1802, Luke Howard classified the different types of clouds. His basic terms were: *cumulus* (meaning heap), *stratus* (meaning layer) and *cirrus* (meaning curl), with various sub-categories. His bright idea of using Latin meant his terms transcended national boundaries, and meteorologists still use his system 200 years later.

Howard also suggested that clouds form for a reason and so founded the science of weather prediction.

DARTS GETS ROYAL APPROVAL

Pubgoers who enjoy a stint at the oche can pinpoint their hobby's worldwide popularity to this day in 1937. Darts had been enjoyed in one form or another for centuries: one theory states that it was first played by archers throwing shortened arrows at the end of a fallen tree.

But it was when King George VI and Queen Elizabeth played an impromptu game while visiting Slough Community Centre that the newspapers seized on the story and darts as a pastime really hit the bullseye.

KING ARTHUR REAWAKENED

The story of King Arthur, with his knights of the round table, wizard-tutor Merlin and chivalric ideals is one of the world's most popular myths. Arthur himself may have existed in the 6th century, but it was today in 1832 that large-scale interest in him was reignited. Alfred, Lord Tennyson, published his famous poem 'The Lady of Shalott', firing the imagination of a Victorian society keen to espouse noble and heroic virtues.

WELCOME TO OUR WORLD

Born as the Empire Service today in 1932, the BBC's famous international broadcasting organisation became known as the World Service in 1965. It is now the world's largest international broadcaster, transmitting news and other programming in 32 languages to 188 million people every week.

THE BEST OF BRITISH BIKES

20 The Nottingham-based Raleigh Cycle Company was founded today in 1887 in the city's Raleigh Street. At first, it made just three bicycles a week, but grew rapidly to become the largest cycle manufacturer in the world, with over 10,000 employees and selling more than a million a year by 1951. Competition came from cheaper cars and foreign cycle manufacturers, but there are still millions of us with happy memories of the first time they sped down the street on a supercool Chopper ...

FIRST CO-OPERATIVE MOVEMENT FOUNDED

21 Co-operative enterprises help people the world over afford goods and services they could not otherwise access. The prototype co-op was The Rochdale Society of Equitable Pioneers, founded today in 1844. A group of 28 weavers and other artisans banded together to open a small store selling quality goods at a price the ordinary man could afford. Within ten years, there were 1,000 co-operatives in the UK.

THE SEWER KING

In the 1850s, the River Thames was the country's largest open sewer. Raw waste also flowed in the streets and 10,000 people would die from cholera in a year. Something had to be done. The Metropolitan Board of Works (founded today in 1855) handed the job to Joseph Bazalgette. His solution was to tear up every street in the city to lay 1,000 miles of local sewers and construct 100 miles of major sewers under new embankments.

And it did the trick: the river came back to life, cholera was wiped out and London had a model sewage system that still works today.

WE'VE GOT THE KNOWLEDGE

London cabbies sometimes get a bit of a rough ride, but 'The Knowledge', the rigorous test of London geographical lore that they must pass, is the world's most demanding training course for taxicab-drivers. Introduced today in 1865, it requires applicants to memorise 25,000 roads and 320 'runs' across town as well as all major places of interest. It usually takes two to four years of zooming round on a moped with an A–Z and 12 attempts at the exam to pass. Where to, Guv?

STUDENTS GRANTED

Cambridge routinely tops the world's best university lists and its graduates dominate the Nobel Prize list with an astonishing 61. Its first college was Peterhouse, and you can trace its history back to this day in 1280 when Edward I first allowed Hugo de Balsham to keep a Master and fourteen 'worthy but impoverished Fellows'. Cambridge's first college had opened its doors.

A STAR WATCHER IS BORN, 1642

Some scientists change the way we look at the world; Isaac Newton changed our perception of the entire universe. His revolutionary *Principia Mathematica* of 1687 sets out his three laws of motion, which form the basis of classical mechanics. It also includes his theory of universal gravitation, which was sparked when he (as legend has it) watched an apple falling from a tree in his orchard. You or I might have picked the apple up and eaten it none the wiser – Newton spent the next twenty years calculating how the apple's descent related to the motion of cosmic bodies, thereby calculating gravity, the universal constant that connects the vastness of space.

MORRIS DANCES BACK TO LIFE

Morris dancing has a history stretching back to the 15th century, but by the end of the 19th century, the tradition was almost extinct. Then today in 1899, folklore enthusiast Cecil Sharp saw a group of morris dancers performing at the village of Headington Quarry. He began collecting the dances and tunes, encouraging a morris revival.

Today, the tradition is thriving, with several hundred dance sides in the UK and many more overseas.

THE INVENTION THAT REALLY CLEANED UP

What should one wipe with? The occupying Romans used sponges on sticks; rags and newspaper have also done the job. But the British Perforated Paper Company was the first to really, ahem, take the matter in hand, when it launched its latest product today in 1880. Paper squares boxed fresh and ready – the first modern loo roll.

PEAK PERFORMANCE

Today in 1950, the Peak District became the United Kingdom's first National Park, protecting 555 square miles of natural beauty and cultural heritage from damaging development. There are over 1,800 miles of public footpaths and long-distance trails in the Peak District, and with an estimated 22 million visitors per year, it is thought to be the second most-visited national park in the world.

DOES IT LOOK LIKE RAIN TO YOU?

Only a Brit could have invented the waterproof coat. Born today in 1766, Charles Macintosh was a chemist who was trying to find uses for the waste products of gasworks when he hit on the notion of painting wool cloth with rubber. Charles Macintosh had just invented the first waterproof coat. Early macs (as they became known, in a nod to their creator) had an alarming tendency to melt in hot weather, but hey, that's not something we Brits have to unduly worry about.

MIND THE GAP

Tower Bridge is one of Britain's most famous icons, and today in 1952 it was the scene of a distinctively British bit of cool thinking. Bus driver Albert Gunter had just started over the bridge when it started to lift. Fearful of either sliding back or trundling into the Thames, Albert promptly slammed his foot to the floor and accelerated, whereupon he, the conductor, ten passengers and the double-decker all leaped the gap. Results: a broken spring for the bus and a £10 bonus to Albert for his quick thinking.

STRICTLY MEDICINAL

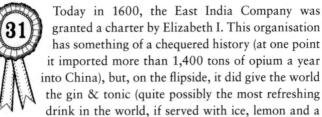

Today in 1600, the East India Company was granted a charter by Elizabeth I. This organisation has something of a chequered history (at one point it imported more than 1,400 tons of opium a year into China), but, on the flipside, it did give the world the gin & tonic (quite possibly the most refreshing drink in the world, if served with ice, lemon and a sprig of mint). Tonic water contains quinine, which the company's officers consumed in large quantities to help prevent against malaria.